MONTH
OF
SUNDAYS

MONTH
OF
SUNDAYS

MELODY MARTIN

KNIGHTSBRIDGE PUBLISHING COMPANY
NEW YORK

Published in the United States by
Knightsbridge Publishing Company
255 East 49th Street
New York, New York 10017

Library of Congress Cataloging-in-Publication Data

Martin, Melody.
  Month of Sundays / Melody Martin.—1st ed.
    p.   cm.
  ISBN 1-877961-70-1 : $18.95
  I. Title.
PS3563.A7263M66   1990
813'.54—dc20   90-35649
                                                                    CIP

Designed by Stanley S. Drate/Folio Graphics Co., Inc.

10 9 8 7 6 5 4 3 2

FIRST EDITION

To my Mother,
Ruth Giffin-Godley,
with love and gratitude.

ACKNOWLEDGMENTS

To my tireless agent Julie Castiglia I extend my heartfelt thanks. To my editor Kate Zentall I second the motion. And to Dan Hare, my housemate, continued gratitude to a good friend.

1

He had not slept well. David rearranged his clothes carefully on the hotel bed as he waited for the water to be just the right temperature for shaving.

He took pains with his appearance. Leaning close to the mirror over the sink, he scrutinized his silent documentary of aging.

Though speckled with gray, he still had good hair. Balding was a loss he found too cruel to contemplate. He ran his anxious fingers through the crown to verify his body's rebellion against shedding.

He noticed one renegade eyebrow hair growing restlessly above the rest. He plucked it, bribed by vanity.

What would he say to these people today? In truth, he had no idea.

By eight he was ready and picking up his car. He called Samantha from the Hertz place.

The phone rang twice before someone picked it up and mumbled a muted hello.

"Sam?"

"Uh-uh; this is Jason."

"Jason. Good morning, son."

He instantly regretted the nervous familiarity. The child on the other end of the phone apparently did not connect. Rock music wafted around as background noise. Jason, undaunted, waited a bit before asking, "Who's this?"

"Jason, it's your—it's David."

"Oh, hi, dude."

"Good morning. Is your mother up?"

"Sure thing."

The phone fell against the counter where Jason tossed it, noncommittally. A resounding thud vibrated in David's ear.

A steady thump of rock rhythms chimed over the wire.

"Hello."

"Good morning, Samantha. I have, as they say, arrived."

"Hello, David. How are you?"

Her voice seemed close, familiar, without the hazy echo of long distance.

"Fine, Sam. And you?"

Ah, the soiled currency of social amenities. Such worn coinage had no place where there had once been passion.

"Listen, David, why don't I just give you the directions and you drive on over. We're not that difficult to find."

"Fair enough."

He copied down the names of Spanish-sounding

streets while she recited lefts and rights. How unnatural the urgent vocabulary of need.

"It should take you about twenty minutes to get here from Westwood. We'll be expecting you."

"Samantha?"

"Yes?" She could feel the muscles in her stomach tighten. This would be a difficult day. Rebecca had already screamed a hateful tirade at Jason, who sat mesmerized in front of the fluorescent flicker of the big-screen Sony. Roger had shouted at both of them, then stormed outside to have a walk before breakfast.

"It's generous of you to let me come."

"David, these are your children too. See you soon."

She hung up without saying good-bye.

The labyrinth of fast lanes and asphalt threw him into a riot of confusion. His rented Buick felt cumbersome and weighty; he rarely drove in Boston except to get away for the weekend. The unfamiliar whir of passing vehicles assaulted his vague uneasiness with premonitions of horrible accidents. He was aware of accelerated motion around him; the speed made him anxious. Normally he was a man who cared about moving fast.

The homes in Santa Monica stood as impressive residences with groomed landscapes oddly lush for such an arid region. The air reeked of kelp and brine. Pushing a button for the automatic windows to open, he heard the dull whine that accompanied the lowering of both windows in the backseat. Currents of sea air whooshed about, blowing his hair from behind. He quickly buzzed the windows up and reached in his pocket for a comb.

He'd forgotten his glasses at the motel. David reminded himself that there are no accidents. He checked himself out in the rear-view mirror. He looked younger without them.

Although he could not read the street signs, it occurred to him that this idyllic neighborhood with its bleached beauty was not a setting for a striking drama. The house on Puebla Drive would be airy and sunny, unlike the macabre streets of the city, winding tributaries of pathos.

He could not imagine living here.

Samantha had changed into a simple sundress and brushed her hair until it fell softly on her shoulders. She was conscious of her desire to look attractive, and part of her sizzled with vague resentment toward everyone.

Her life had been symmetrical until his plaintive phone call a month ago. The strains of his doleful voice had alarmed her, even after all that time, with the poignancy of his plea.

She genuinely pitied him. She wondered if he'd aged well, aware that old lovers put time clocks on each other. She would be forty in October. She'd faced her thirtieth birthday alone. David had left three weeks before. She'd celebrated that milestone alone in her apartment, reading *Where the Wild Things Are* to her children and wondering if David would come back from what she'd vainly deluded herself into thinking was a temporary exit born of a midlife crisis.

But she'd known better. In her more lucid moments she knew she was on her own, and it had been terrible. From her safely edited memory calendar, Samantha would generously comfort her younger colleagues concerned about maturing with a lighthearted "Thirty is highly overrated as a depressant," a conviction she almost believed.

Roger was washing the car. He took pleasure in the languid rituals of the weekend, where his sense of time could be dictated by the lull of his senses, the sun, or desire. Unlike his coworkers at Pacific Mutual Insurance, he looked forward to going home at the end of the day. Roger and Jason would eagerly head for the ocean to catch the last waves before the sun went down.

"Oldest adolescent I know" was the frequent critique tossed around half-jokingly by his own friends and colleagues. And Roger would confirm it further.

"I grew up on the beach, and it's part of my life. I need the water."

He said that with no irony whatsoever. He called himself a simple man who knew what he liked. Roger's concept of the good life had been forged in high school. He wanted the beach and the sun, conservative politics, a good woman, a good job, a couple of kids, and enough money to stay in Southern California. He'd never been to Europe, although once he was offered a chance to be an exchange student, but had turned it down.

"No waves in Germany. Now, if you offered Australia, we'd talk."

He'd majored in business at USC, got good grades, joined Sigma Alpha Epsilon, and in his junior year fell desperately in love with Suzy Willis, a blond and beautiful runner-up for Rose Bowl Queen.

They married two weeks after graduation, and he began his career at the Pasadena branch of Pacific Mutual. They'd rented a small house at the beach, and life had been good. He'd counted on that. What he'd failed to see was that little Suzy's party-girl gaiety masked a drinking problem that would remain unacknowledged, despite two 502s and frequent blackouts dismissed as migraines, until she smashed herself to smithereens on the Ventura Freeway, totaling her new Mustang and one-half mile of road dividers. The coroner had ordered an autopsy and found that her body contained enough blood alcohol "to pickle a pack of pythons."

She died at ten o'clock in the morning. And since memory was his fraudulent bookkeeper, he'd pushed this account to the back of his head and buried her and mourned her as a sudden, tragic loss. It wasn't until years later that he would look back on the romance with a sense of remorse and guilt.

He'd become a playboy after her death, although his rather wholesome adaption to boulevardier caused ripples of amused compassion in his partners, whose sexual daring had surpassed his in puberty. He transferred to Hawaii for a year for a change of scenery and bigger waves. But he sank deeper into bleak depression.

A brief affair with a surfing social worker convinced him that his desire to skim along the surface could prevent him from being happy, a state he'd assumed was his birthright and had never questioned. He told her about Suzy; it was the first time he'd told the story out loud.

"She was an alcoholic, then?" she inquired matter-of-factly.

"Yes, I suppose."

"It's too bad she didn't get help before she killed herself." Her words had pelted his heart like snowballs tossed against chapped skin.

He cried for Suzy and for himself, and she gave him the name of a colleague in L.A. who would help him fumigate his closet of sadness.

He moved stateside in a month, and then went to Dr. Saperstein's office on Camden Drive, anxious about what would actually take place. Psychologists had always been shrinks or expanders in his book, completely unnecessary wastes of time except for those poor fools at the precipice of insanity.

He jumped as the door opened and Dr. Saperstein escorted out a fair-haired lady who'd obviously been crying. A fragile blond boy of about five held her hand. Behind her, a morose and whiny girl kicked at the carpet and grabbed her mother's skirt.

Roger stood up in confusion, but the doctor did not acknowledge him just then. The dark and petulant girl walked up to him and for no apparent reason socked him squarely in the scrotum.

Later he would chide Samantha about their first encounter.

"Took my breath away, sugar."

He was here. Shaking hands with Roger.

Disquieting and strange portrait, the two of them. She gazed from the window, absorbing frame by frame this anxious melodrama.

He looked the same, only older.

She had read once that in first love, young girls gave themselves to their lovers; in later loves, love merely came to them.

The men climbed the outside steps together; as if in slow motion she watched them rise, in unison, with each step.

She went to find the children.

David's voice filled the living room, rich and resonant tones of false mirth and forced pleasantries.

"Jason, David is here."

"Far out."

She knocked on Rebecca's door.

"He's here."

"Be still, my beating heart."

"Come out and say hello, right now!"

"I'll be there in a minute."

She walked into the living room with Jason, carefully avoiding his stare.

"Hello, David," she offered casually, a poignant knot tightening in her stomach.

He forced himself to exhale, slowly.

"Samantha, it's lovely to see you."

The moment ached with stiffness. Samantha touched her son's head.

"And this is Jason," she offered, in an awkward introduction of mottled feelings.

"Hey, dude."

Jason smiled a genuine grin and stuck out his hand, which David clasped like a lifeline.

Welcome me, David's eyes pleaded to Samantha, who nervously fingered the pockets of her sundress.

"Why don't we sit and have some coffee?" Roger offered, the voice of the rational outsider. Roger could always be counted on to do the right thing to ease tension, even though the whole situation pissed him off.

"Honey, where's Rebecca?"

"Right here," she echoed from the doorway, and four heads turned to stare.

No one was prepared for the grotesque vision posed there, dressed in her mother's black cocktail dress, made up like a transsexual with blood-red lips outlined in dark pencil, eyes wildly exaggerated with deep gashes of multicolored shadow, cheeks flaming sun-balls against pale skin. Costume jewelry dangled from every appendage, swaying in staccato jerks as she sashayed across the floor in needle-point heels, her hand extended like a fading countess's.

"David, how nice of you to drop in. I wanted to be properly attired so my East Coast father wouldn't feel out of place."

She shook his hand coldly. No one spoke.

2

He absorbed each detail carefully, one at a time, so the im-
print would remain fixed.

Accoutrements of the good life surrounded him,
amused him with their satiric potential, pained him with
the confirmation that he did not belong. He scanned the
kitchen counter as Samantha made coffee and Roger
uttered banalities about current events.

They had once mocked modern conveniences and
conspicuous consumption, writhing in disdain for those
poor Babbitts who needed objects to clutter up the existential void.

Focused on the Mixmaster, his eyes moved to the
Cuisinart, the juicer, a coffee-bean grinder, a dutch oven,
and the microwave.

A labyrinth of wires and extension cords snaked

their way up the yellow ceramic tile like ungroomed bougainvillea on a neglected trellis.

A woman of passion who pushed buttons marked GRATE and MINCE.

He would joke about such items with his students.

"Imagine, if you will, Anna Karenina slouched across her Maytag, rhapsodizing over the permanent-press cycle. Vronsky envelops her in his arms and testifies that his little woman knows how to handle things around the house, and just to make sure, she inserts one Geritol capsule into her esophagus at exactly eight o'clock Eastern Standard Time."

Samantha guessed what he was thinking; his silences had always conveyed weighty messages. Shoving the plug to the percolator into the socket, she caught his eye and flickered a faint How dare you.

He understood and smiled at their unchanged intimacy. She looked out the window.

"David, I'm sorry about Rebecca. I didn't know she'd do that."

"Let's just say she greeted my presence with something less than unequivocal joy."

She gave him a look signifying You'll-never-understand-that-she's-hurt, but she refrained from saying it aloud to him. He caught it anyway.

"Apparently, Rebecca is of the age at which hostility is a rather normal tenet of human interaction."

"She's just pissed that you're here," Jason piped out, spewing a spray of peanut butter as he hit the implosive *p*. David wiped the sticky, tan dots from his sleeve.

"Sorry, dude."

"Well, I'm sorry she's so upset. Do you want to talk to her, Sam?"

The perk of the coffee sputtered and gurgled in

steamy bursts of fragrant odor. Sam smoothed her hair away from her face, a gesture so familiar that both men registered it immediately.

"Jason, go tell your sister to hurry up."

"Do I have to?"

"Now."

She waited until he had left, trailing a string of protests along the way. She peered at Roger for reassurance and then spoke softly but distinctly.

"David, I'm not going to run interference between you and the kids. If you think she needs talking to, then you do it. You have a lot to explain to her anyway."

A trace of hostility tinged her words. She fought to regain control. She meant what she said. Roger shifted nervously, scratching his face, which did not itch.

"Would you two like me to leave?" Roger had no intention of leaving.

"No," she snapped a bit too quickly. "Stay here, Roger; this isn't a fight. I told him that I could not guarantee reactions or behaviors. That was part of the deal."

David sighed heavily, contemplating the madness of his decision to be here. The sunlight danced in her hair, lithe strands falling like jagged cornsilk onto the sensuous slope of her neck.

The sight of her put his sexual instinct on alert. He basked in the inappropriateness of his desire.

"Where are you taking them?" Roger inquired inoffensively.

"I thought we'd go to Disneyland."

"Today?"

"Sure; why?"

"It's a bit of a distance from here. And it's summer;

you need to get an early start." The brilliant scholar had a practical IQ of zero, Roger mused.

"I loathe Disneyland." Rebecca ambled into the kitchen, smelling of Dial soap and toothpaste. Traces of pink friction lined her face where she had scrubbed off her war paint. A cascade of wavy chestnut hair fell languidly down her back. She appeared younger than he'd expected, more interesting than pretty, but her forehead had an introspective allure, like his own. Her eyes sizzled with impatience.

"You don't like Disneyland, Rebecca?" His tone resonated with the patronizing patience often affected by adults speaking to children. She bristled with annoyance and spoke directly into his face.

"Disneyland is a repository of vulgarity for white trash who lack imagination."

"Rebecca!" Sam snapped, but Jason outshouted her.

"Aw, man, don't listen to her. Disneyland rules!"

"Rules what?" David asked honestly.

"Rules his saline-flooded frontal lobes," Rebecca sneered.

"Cram it, dog."

Roger told them both to shut up.

David sought out Sam's gaze, but she busied herself pouring coffee.

You're on your own, she thought to herself, with no small infusion of satisfaction.

"Cream and sugar, David?"

"Black, thanks." His politeness was edged with irritation at her having forgotten this kind of detail.

"Well, if it's too late for Disneyland, we'll cook up some other kind of adventure."

"I can't wait."

"Rebecca," Roger said, placing a firm hand on her forearm, "a bit of common courtesy wouldn't kill you."

She did not answer him.

"Good coffee, Samantha."

She caught his irony and let it pass.

"Well, where are we going?" Rebecca inquired with exasperation. Jason had a suggestion.

"Why don't we go to the skateboard park in Venice?"

"I'd rather have cancer," his sister sneered.

"That bad, eh? What, pray tell, is a skateboard park?"

"Don't they do that back East?" Rebecca's curiosity was piqued.

"Do what?"

"Ride around on a board with wheels in an empty swimming pool. Wear crash helmets and knee pads and shriek and grunt like retarded pigs."

Jason jumped up, angry.

"No way, Alpo queen, it shreds. She doesn't know what's going down."

"What's 'shreds'?" he asked. Roger offered the translation.

"That means exciting. You'll get used to this language soon enough. We've given up trying to compete with plain English."

"If you ask me, he's just inarticulate and stupid, like the rest of his lodie friends."

"No one asked you," Roger informed her.

"Do I have to wear shoes?" Jason whined.

"Yes," Samantha insisted, explaining to David that no one's kids wore footwear out here. Rubber thongs were sold at the high school because so many kids showed up barefoot, and the law required that students wear shoes.

He was bored by this information but attempted not to show it.

"Hey, dude, will we be back in time for *Family Ties?*"

"Gimme a break, Jason," his sister muttered.

"I assume it's a favorite TV show?" David riveted his quizzical stare on Samantha. His eyes were critical and questioning.

"If you haven't seen that one, David, you're culturally deprived," she said, curling her upper lip into a half-sneer.

"I don't own a television set."

Roger laughed good-naturedly.

"We own four of them."

Samantha wished he hadn't said that.

"Shall we get moving, then?" David rose and put his cup in the sink.

Samantha noticed.

"I'm gonna get a book."

"Fair enough, Rebecca. Jason, are you ready?"

"Sure. Let's bail."

"You'll have to wait a minute. Rebecca went to get a book."

"Let's bail, man—she's stalling. You'll learn."

He was confused, but moved toward the living room to collect his jacket. The morning air blew Samantha's scent about him. How quickly we recapture the familiar, he thought to himself, as he noted the cheerfulness of the furniture and carefully placed objects bending toward optimism.

Rebecca slouched in, book in hand, a nylon backpack slung lazily over one shoulder.

"You going camping?" David joked. She didn't laugh.

"Purses are for preps."

"I see," he said, not seeing at all. "Shall we?"

Roger and Samantha stood side by side, an oddly tan and organic version of *American Gothic.*

They looked like they belonged together. He wondered if they moaned in bed, thrashed around in heated frenzies, sweating bodies grinding toward Bethlehem enveloped in percale sheets.

He knew she could be moved to sigh and scream; did this robust stranger share that with her?

"We'll be home in the early evening."

"Good. It's a school night." Then she laughed nervously, realizing it was summer and it didn't matter when they got to bed.

She felt the faint throb of a headache beginning at the base of her neck. She reached up to massage it gently, hoping to divert the potential waste of the afternoon.

"Roger . . . Sam, thank you both for this opportunity."

And like a salesman making a final pitch before his exit, he shook both of their hands.

Jason charged down the stairs, and Rebecca sighed loudly and demanded the front seat.

"Aw, mellow in," Jason chimed in from the backseat.

David turned on the ignition and waited for the muted grind of the engine to take on a regular rhythm. He backed out slowly, cautiously, aware of critical eyes and judgmental nods around him.

The car stalled.

His children choked him with their silence. The warming engine sent a tremor through the Buick.

"What are you reading, Rebecca?"

She looked up from her book, irritated.

"For Whom the Bell Tolls."

"You like Hemingway?"

"He's okay."

"Who's he?" Jason demanded.

"Forget it, you'd hate him."

"Actually," David ventured, "I've done a bit of work on him."

"I know."

"In fact, I wrote a book about it."

"I read it," she sighed out the window to the palm trees lining the sidewalk.

"And?" David queried.

"You're as macho as he is, and you use too many adverbs."

"He's a nice enough fellow, I suppose."

Samantha hurriedly picked up the kitchen, anxious to restore order.

"Rebecca's going to give him a run for his money."

She didn't answer him, except to give a slight shrug to her shoulders.

"Jason's all right, don't you think, Sam?"

"Sure." A muffled affirmation; she did not feel like discussing David. Roger slid in behind her, pressing the weight of his pelvis against the crease of her buttocks. She felt his stiffness, a pointed dagger, throbbing, ready, a lover's lance so quickly aroused by a kiss or a look. His steamy breath warmed her neck.

"Did he upset you?"

"Not especially." That was a lie. Seeing him gave rise

to a hail of conflicting emotions. He still possessed that magnetic charm, and she hated him for it.

"I'll take your mind off him," he whispered, and cupped his palm around the fleshy firmness of her breast.

"Please, Roger, not now, okay?"

He pulled away from her, slowly releasing the pressure of his body weight against the folds of white cotton. A curved indentation marked the spot where his love had been offered—empty, concave space.

"I really do have a headache," she echoed, realizing how silly that sounded. She felt guilty and wondered if she should change her mind, but she couldn't. Her feelings were in a turmoil.

"Right."

He left the room noisily, his signal for anger that would subside in a while and be assimilated into some form of vigorous activity, used up, dispersed, spent, forgotten.

It had taken a long time for Samantha to become accustomed to his strange and frenzied ways of coping.

Pensive, brooding silence—that was the tool of hate and fear. Grinding obsessions mulled over for days, lacerated by sneering sarcasm rubbed into festering wounds until someone screamed for a reprieve. Icy, rigid gestures, infused with aggressive innuendo; a sharp turn of the tongue cleverly placed to make one clean cut—those weapons belonged to David, and she had grown used to them.

Roger shouted and ran, or else he yelled and washed the car, rode the waves, or tossed a Frisbee. And then it was over.

With David, it was never over. She feared that was the problem now.

The bobbing silhouette of Roger moved like heat

waves wafting off the sand. She could trace the path of his jog from the kitchen window.

In the beginning she had judged him simple, uncomplex, a man who dared not look too deeply.

She no longer felt this was true.

He'd decided to take them out for brunch and drove into town to a restaurant resembling a shipwrecked schooner in Marina del Rey. Nets and crystal balls were draped along the staircase made to look like a ship's ladder, sprinkled with decorative seashells to create an illusion of being underwater. The waitresses wore nautical mini-dresses. They eyed David with no special interest; he was just another Sunday father who would leave a generous tip in exchange for nurturing service and an amiable presence that would make conversation easier.

"Why don't we begin with eggs Benedict?" David suggested.

"I'm allergic to eggs," Rebecca snipped.

"Since when?"

"Birth."

Indeed, he had forgotten.

"Why don't you kids just order what you'd like."

Jason smiled at the waitress and rattled off a list of requests.

"You eat pretty good, don't you, son?" she chirped, writing it down. Her insensitivity to grammar offended him, but he said nothing. Rebecca cringed and put in her order.

"You guys have a nice day, okay?"

"Sure thing, cookie," Rebecca mumbled when she was out of earshot. "It's the sincerity that kills you, n'est-ce pas?"

"Do you speak French, Rebecca?" He was genuinely interested.

"Perhaps. Why?"

"I simply wondered if you shared my love of languages." He wanted to slap her.

"I hate languages," Jason offered. "Spanish is such a bummer, but I copied off of Lance and got a 'D.' "

"Jason," David leaned toward this tan and exuberant boy wolfing down huge chunks of bread and butter. "What exactly do you like?"

He talked with his mouth full, an appalling spectacle to someone unschooled in the observation of such flaws of etiquette.

"Surfing, skateboarding, TV, my friends, my dad, lobster."

"I see."

"He's a real tower of intellect, don't you think?" sniffed Rebecca.

Jason kicked her with his high-tops, each a different color—"the radical, ultimate killer shoes," he had explained to David in the car, while balancing his feet on the headrest for emphasis.

David chose to ignore the assault under the table.

"And you, if memory serves me correctly, are rather partial to books."

"Your memory is more reliable than your presence, isn't it?"

This was going to be a long day.

She hiked down to the beach to wait for him, a can of Coors tucked in each pocket, chilled and wet against her thighs. The sand crept between her toes like slithery moon dust, soft and grainy.

She sat down near the water's edge, where the cool

spray of the shore-break would sprinkle its salty freshness over her. Sandpipers picked around, ignoring the guttural chirp of noisy seagulls nose-diving into the shallow water, snatching the flesh of some hapless fish winnowing around in the warm water. Couples walked along in sync to the rhythm of the breaking waves; children played in the sand, digging up unexpected treasures while parents breathed in the sun with a pleasant lassitude and a minimum of conversation.

It was lovely here.

She would be more grateful.

It was David's sense of gratitude that had captivated her tormented soul during her junior year at Mount Holyoke. She'd heard about his ruthless reputation just like every other coed had, but she was simply too numb from her mother's suicide to be terribly interested. She buried her sorrow in Poussin and Degas, spending endless hours thumbing through the stacks of oversized books containing works of beauty that would live on forever, unlike her mother. She sought solace in the gentle beauty of Mount Holyoke, where her mother had also studied. Samantha had been accepted on an alumni scholarship so generously supported by successful former graduates. Her mother's life had not turned out as planned. She'd married John Peterson, banker and graduate of the University of Massachusetts, and moved to New York full of resolve to make it as a painter in the art world of Manhattan. Samantha was planned and wanted. Her early childhood recollections were happy images of Rockefeller Center and strolls down Madison Avenue to ogle the elaborate Christmas decorations and watch the fancy people who lived uptown. John Peterson dropped dead on the floor of the Chase Manhattan Bank on Wall Street, felled by a massive heart attack no one could have predicted. Samantha was barely five. She and her mother moved out of the city to Hastings-on-Hudson into a tiny house surrounded by birch trees and the endless flow of falling leaves. Her mother continued to paint in the garage she had converted to a quasi-studio. Samantha would visit there after school just to be in the same room with her. Sometimes they wouldn't talk at all. Her mother would hand her a sketch pad and a pencil and simply say, "Draw something."

Samantha learned to paint and draw in the silent garage on Villard Lane. She was a shy and introspective girl, fragile and pretty to the careful observer, but essentially unnoticed, especially in high school, where strident and energetic girls gained popularity by vigor and pep and a willingness to cheer teams on to victory and build endless floats from crepe paper and chicken wire. Samantha's art teacher recognized her talent and encouraged her to enter art contests in the city. She never did. All she solicited was her mother's approval, which was given in sporadic spurts, uttered in measured terms and treasured like prayers. She didn't really want to go to college, not from a lack of desire but from fear of leaving home. Though silence was the general tenor of the household, Samantha secretly insisted to herself that her presence was essential to her mother's well-being.

She entered Mount Holyoke as an anxious, reluctant freshman who spent most of her scholarship money on phone calls to Hastings and train tickets home whenever the opportunity arose. She was aware of her mother's increasing withdrawal from the world, and it caused endless waves of worry each time she had to return to South Hadley. She made a few friends and lost herself in the stacks, gazing at art book after art book, seeking answers to questions she herself could not articulate.

During the summer between her sophomore and junior years, Samantha took a job in a bakery near the train station in Hastings. She sold jelly rolls and cinnamon buns to harried matrons who took no notice of the dread terror in her eyes as she ran five sorts of bread through the automatic slicer and gave change like it was hot metal.

Samantha found her in mid August, slumped in a tattered easy chair in her studio. Samantha knew she was dead before she could muster the courage to verify it. The scent of flour commingled with the pungent odor of oil-base paint still wet on an unfinished canvas. Samantha stood there and stared for two hours before she phoned the police and the undertaker. She sketched her mother in ebony charcoal, making sure of the exactitude of the lines in her hands, the correct slope of her neck and folds of her skirt. Her finished tableau bore an eerie resemblance to a Mary Cassatt, trying to recapture the bone weariness of a woman who dedicated her days to the rearing of children and the deadening regularity of domesticity.

Overdose of Seconal was the official cause of death, but Samantha knew that the real culprit was a simple desire to stop living in a world wrapped in gauze. She tended to the details with a crisp and efficient dedication, closed up the house, and returned to school in the fall, numb as gums shot full of novocaine, and wandered through her classes like a walking candle until the unexpected venom of David Bartholomew brought her smoldering grief to the surface in one explosive gush of uncontrollable sobs.

He'd apologized to her in the empty classroom, but his words were like hollow echoes down empty corridors. He'd sent her flowers, and notes filled with remorse, which she regarded with detached sentiment, though every coed in her dorm was stupefied that someone had penetrated his armor.

Samantha scarcely noticed.

She did not speak in class, and he did not single her out for humiliation. Her presence in the room softened him, toned him down to the point at which words like *compassion* and *empathy* crept into his lectures where sour, stinging nouns had once danced. His hesitant, conscientious restraint was marked by everyone save Samantha.

"Miss Peterson, would you kindly stay after class? I'd like a word with you," he braved one fall afternoon.

She remained in her seat while the rest of the class slithered out of the door, exchanging hushed whispers.

He approached her cautiously.

"Samantha," he said gently, "I'd like to tell you something."

She did not respond. He continued anyway.

"My father left before I was born. I wallowed in sorrow for years. I searched for him, yearned for him with such fervor that I do not want you to misinterpret that I am a man without a heart."

She traced his face for irony, but found none.

"Essentially it all boiled down to this: There are the because-ofs and the in-spite-ofs. Clearly I am the latter. I think you are the former."

"What is that supposed to mean?" she asked bitterly.

"I think you are who you are because of your mother. All in all, that's not such an unfair base, all things considered."

"And you? What are you?"

"A person who's dedicated his life to pleasing a ghost, an indifferent ghost."

"You've built a kingdom around you where you wound others," she accused.

"Yes," he whispered, adding, "it is a sad and lonely terrain, Samantha. You have made me see just how empty a walled fortress can be."

She listened cautiously, waiting for her distrust to give her back her defenses.

"I would like to know you better. I think we can offer each other some essentials that have nothing to do with books or paintings."

She listened quietly.

"I would like to have feelings for something, and I think you can help me open that door."

"I don't feel anything," she confessed spontaneously.

"I suspected as much. Let me help you refine that."

"How?"

"Let's begin with a ride on a beautiful autumn day. We'll go to Jacob's Pillow and get a perspective on this valley."

They drove in silence up the winding, narrow road of Jacob's Ladder, serpentining to the top of the wooded mountain. The colors of autumn were deep and rich, and the air smelled of rain and freshly dug earth. He pulled over by the enormous rock shaped like a pillow resting majestically at the summit.

They strolled through the dank forest, still damp from morning dew. Leaves of all shapes and hues covered the earth like multicolored linen.

He told her about his father, his past so carefully ordered by his mother, Nervy Nellie, the librarian who fought for freedom of the press and raised her son alone. He made candlelight promises to Samantha of a life hereafter. His words softened her fears, and she listened to his sadness pour out its lonely tale amidst the elms and oaks that would keep their secrets.

She told him about her mother, recounting every detail of her death day as it flooded back with such alarming accuracy.

She did not cry. He did. He cried for her, for himself, for the world so full of sadness and devoid of substantial meaning.

She watched him sob without words of mourning, letting the heaves of his chest mark time and space that made no sense.

She moved toward him like a magnet and put her arms gently around him, burying her face in his neck. They stood there for a long time in the merciful caress of condolence. They tightened their grasp like ruling life-lines, then broke away to survey the emotional road maps of each other's face, which announced a beginning that both of them accepted with no small amount of trepidation and hope.

It happened quickly, much faster than either one could have predicted. Side trips to Sturbridge and Deer-field wound up as extended weekends of passion and pathos so profound in intensity that neither could eat or sleep much for days afterward.

They made love in candlelight, at dawn, and at the close of the day.

He begged her to stay with him forever.

She promised that she would.

Nervy Nellie rejoiced and welcomed Samantha as yet another blessing in the plan of the Almighty.

They were married at Saint Andrew's on Easter morning of Samantha's senior year. It was 1971, and they were full of optimism. Her side of the church contained no one save the scattered members of the congregation sensitive enough to fill in the empty spaces.

Samantha was a beautiful bride of such wistful loveliness that David's voice faltered with emotion as he repeated his vows. She smelled like lilies of the valley, and her eyes radiated reflection of hope, love, and joy enveloped in the snowy cascade of illusion lace that covered her head like angel hair.

The vision of his very own Griselda was etched into his memory bank forever, carved as the ultimate representation of all that was holy and his.

They bowed their heads for the blessings of the minister. And they listened with the intensity of the newly enamored for whom solemnity of promise is as vital as air:

> Bestow on them, if it is your will, the gift and heritage of children, and the grace to bring them up to know You, to love You, and to serve You. Amen.

The words sent frissons of happiness through Samantha's gauzy dreams. Visions of babies in white satin christening robes danced in her imagination as she pictured Christmas trees surrounded by children's toys, music boxes that trilled lullabies, the sweet perfume of baby talc, and the sensation of an infant's velvet skin pressed up against her heart. They would be a real family, like the Kennedys, with picnics and football games, and she would raise them to know God.

David's body stiffened as the minister spoke of the gift of children. The words burned into his happiness like hot branding irons. Samantha was his soul mate, his redeemer in lost ideals of lofty emotion, private joy. She was his secret harbinger of a happiness of such hermetically sealed intensity that the very idea of sharing her sent chills of dread through his grateful, bursting heart.

They exchanged misty glances and gold rings and promised to love and comfort, honor and keep, forsake others and be faithful, as long as they both should live.

And each of them meant it from the hollow caverns of hearts that had been broken and that could now mend each other and heal from within.

David kissed his bride the way the reverent ones embrace the foot of the Pieta.

"I could die happy now," Nellie announced to no one in particular. And two months later, three days before Samantha's graduation, Nellie had a massive coronary in the town library, where she volunteered twice a week. She fell in one resounding thud in front of the biographies, witnessed only by a random, gasping thirteen-year-old searching for a worthy subject for a term paper.

The Bartholomews buried Nellie to the strains of Mozart's twentieth piano concerto. Samantha sensed that she had lost a person who would have grown to be an ally in times of trouble, but she braved it out for David's sake, stood by his side and was strong for him.

"It's just the two of us now," he said in solemn tranquility, and then wrapped himself around her like a warm quilt.

They clung to each other like enamored adolescents, unwilling to share any part with the outside world lest it rob them of some valuable, inexplicable part that neither could articulate but both coveted greedily.

They moved to Boston, where David became a professor of literature at Boston University, and they settled into a life of domestic bliss so intensely separated from the outside world that neither could bear the idea of the intrusion of the mundane or the clutter of trivial concerns.

They had each other, and that was all that mattered until Samantha began to feel the stirrings of maternal urgency and slowly suggested to David that they make a baby as a mark of their love.

The thought horrified him, and his reaction was so strong that Samantha feared he did not love her. She pleaded with him, which only served to make him all the more insistent of the specialness of their union, which he treasured above all else.

They had wonderful fun together, traipsing off on wild weekends born of spur-of-the-moment decisions. David showered her with small gifts—flowers, perfume, love poems, and exotic jewelry bought from street vendors in Cambridge. He would call her at unexpected hours of the day just to tell her how much he loved and cherished her. His words thrilled her, but the ache to have a child gnawed at her.

Living in Boylston had been fine at first, but the sight of ladies in the park pushing prams saddened Samantha. She wanted children, and it struck her as abnormal that David did not. She had it all worked out in a fantasy. She would take the MTA into town and meet him for a Cuba Libre at the Old Oyster House and tell him her good news. He would toast his joy and insist they celebrate by dining at Loch Ober's or Parker House, finances be damned.

But that was not how it finally turned out. He accused her of tricking him and insisted that they have it taken care of. Samantha would hear of no such thing. She wanted this baby, no matter what.

She felt the cool breeze off the Pacific lift her hair from her shoulders. The California coast was so beautiful, and her life here was so complete, compared with then.

At this time of year, Boston would be a sweltering sewer of heavy heat and muggy moodiness. People would hover by the air conditioner or seek refuge in a climatized bar or shop. The less fortunate would hang out the window or climb to the terrace in search of a whisper of a breeze, sullied by the dust on the streets and the odors of living packed in.

When David started his career at B.U., they'd roamed the neighborhoods of Boston like dauntless vagabonds, exploring the streets of Cambridge and downtown, stopping at Scollay Square for a drink or a bite to eat. Impulse dictated the rhythm of their life together. They would dash off to Revere Beach to spend the night, or else walk around Beacon Hill to observe how rich people lived.

Then Rebecca came. David grew sullen, irritable, infested with dark passions that led him to stay up all night reading bleak novels and sardonic articles crucifying modern fiction, the theater, poetry. He became obsessed with publishing papers on metaphor in Marx, the vision of Poe, the sensitivity of allusion of Austen. She got them all mixed up, since they dovetailed with one another in impact and intensity. She loved Rebecca with a fearful dread; the more effusive she was to her child, the more distant he'd become.

She tried to get a master's in art from Boston College, but the time away from home cost her too dearly. David begged her to leave Rebecca with a friend and spend the summer traveling in Europe with him. Samantha could not leave Rebecca for three months; she refused.

He flew into a rage, ripping art books to shreds and heaving the remnants about like glossy snowflakes.

He shrieked that he loved her from the depth and

could not bear to share her with diapers, formulas, and infantile chatter.

She cried all night, and Rebecca wailed, and at dawn he came to her remorseful and they made love, and as a result, Jason.

From then on the streets of Boston became ugly, filthy tunnels to her, avenues where you walked fussy children in the dirty air and hoped they would not tread through dog shit or wino vomit or witness some pervert's playtime or a random act of human cruelty that was daily street theater there. She despised the chatter of ethnic tongues, the swagger of the homosexual, the defeated faces of mothers in the park. David rarely came home; when he did it was to torment her and ignore the children, or sometimes he would stay long enough to spew a spleen-riddled tirade on the death of love that was somehow supposed to be her fault.

She was not surprised when he left.

Still, she despaired.

A jouncy figure shuffled into view. Roger's graceful gait could be spotted from far away—the evenness of this stride, his head held back and high, arms resting taut at his side. The breeze blew his hair straight back as if it were trying for the Wall Street chic so popular now in L.A.

He saw her sitting there and slackened his pace to cool down. She walked over to him, dug in her pocket, and handed him her peace offering.

"Fuck him, Roger."

"I'd rather fuck you."

Brunch had turned into a tiresome fiasco of strained dialogue and sibling rivalry. David found himself in the role of mediator and defensive guard.

He didn't like either very much.

He wasn't completely sure he liked these children.

Jason posed a perplexing portrait, faintly disturbing to a man like David accustomed to highly verbal children, street-wise and sophisticated. Apparently this child found all forms of education tedious, especially books, which made him tired. Writing anything proved taxing to the point of exhaustion, and yet his raw enthusiasm drew David to him. David was aware of a desire to be physically close to this boy, to caress his hair as he laughed in unsullied spurts or share his joy at some spontaneous observation of a passerby.

Jason was glad to be with him. David felt that and wanted to thank him for it.

Rebecca disturbed him. Capricious and bright, David sensed in her so many trembling layers of fear and loathing that to wade through the arsenal of hostility would take months, even years, of unconditional love and patience.

He possessed neither.

And yet he was drawn to her from a different direction. There was a volatile passion in that child, a sadness whose undercurrent suggested deep and lonely caverns where dark secrets lay dormant, and dreams fermented like cauldrons of bubbling poison. The brittle edges of her pointed rhetoric amused and infuriated him with their studied accuracy and clarity.

She resented his presence utterly.

She needed him more than Jason did.

He surmised that she would wound and be wounded frequently in her life.

She was not a happy child.

They drove home in silence, having exhausted the liaisons of commonality long before and replaced them with a sort of information-gathering bout of twenty questions. He interrogated both as to their likes and dislikes, school events, and observations of the world around them.

He offered them a chance to query him. Jason posed an avalanche of harmless questions that he answered directly and by anecdote, coloring occasional details with small exaggerations and lies to appear more interesting.

Rebecca moped in moody silence.

The house was a welcome beacon; he was glad they had a place to go.

"I guess I'll see you next Sunday, kids."

"Sure, dude, it's been real. Later."

Jason slammed the door and walked up the stairs. Rebecca hugged the handle but did not move.

"Thank you for spending your Sunday with me, Rebecca."

"Yeah. I really had a choice."

"Well, so be it, I still thank you."

"If you're so hot to see us, why did you dump us in the first place?"

She left before he could tell her he had no concise answer.

4 The following day, David returned to his hotel room from a walk to find his telephone light blinking. A message was waiting for him down at the office. David pondered this. It was unlikely that someone from work would have called him, since he'd mentioned his destination only to Elizabeth, and even she had no idea where he'd be staying.

Elizabeth was the woman who'd survived the tenuous transition of lover to friend.

Perhaps it was because their love affair had stemmed from the roots of loneliness each had felt for different reasons that bleakly cold winter of '80. A survivor of the '60s in Berkeley, Chicago, and Alabama, Elizabeth had set aside plastiques and pickets to resign herself to disillusioned idealism by teaching French literature to Boston beauties and watching her husband, Jed, wither away from some rare type of bone cancer.

David had noticed her straightaway when she joined the faculty. He'd studied and observed her movements for clues to her opinion of him.

She rarely spoke to anyone except her students, who found her animated, cynical, and a bit tough on the grading of a blue book. He'd tried like hell to engage her in conversations about Ronsard, Rousseau, rock 'n' roll. She'd avoided him utterly until one day when she could no longer. He had her cornered by the ancient Ditto machine in the faculty workroom. He had planned a humorous monologue on why pathetic fallacies transcended nationalism in literature, but she cut him off before he had the chance to commence.

"Before you say something you'll come to regret, let me tell you that I know all about you and your harassment hard-ons, and frankly the idea of a colleague who needs to fuck freshmen strikes me as somewhat of a cliché, not to mention makes me want to puke."

She shoved a fresh load of paper into the Ditto machine and changed carbons without once looking up.

"Besides, rumor has it that your work has nosedived into that cozy quagmire of mediocrity brought on by the guidance of the gonads. And finally, Mr. Bartholomew, I don't trouble myself with people who have more problems than I do."

And she ripped the stencil from its stainless steel cylinder, gathered her midterms, and left him standing speechless and aroused.

Of course he had to have her.

His excuse came sooner than expected. The new *M.L.A. Style Sheet* arrived in the middle of a blizzard. Elizabeth's article, "Balzac as a Social Chronicler," had been moved up to appear in this issue. He seized the opportunity to discover where she lived so he could hand-deliver a copy to her, since she'd told the department secretary she would be out all week due to illness.

He'd merely assumed it was her own.

She lived, to his delight, quite close to him on the west side, off Charles Avenue. The building was a huge cement edifice, one of those urban renewal projects that mixed and matched black and white, old and young, rich and poor. Culinary odors lingered in the hallways, and the melodious clacking of foreign tongues echoed off the stucco walls.

She looked tired and surprised to see him. Strange smells oozed from inside her apartment, the pungent perfume of the sick chamber, the fumes of rubbing alcohol and despair.

She let him in hesitantly, where they sat in her tasteful but sterile living room and talked as parodies of themselves. A buxom woman in her fifties waddled into the room to the regular rhythm of the swish of her white uniform.

"He's resting comfortably now. I'm going to leave, if that's okay by you. His next injection is around nine. I left the syringe ready on the table."

"Thank you, Mrs. Cooper. I'll see you in the morning."

Elizabeth showed her to the door and returned without offering an explanation.

They talked pleasantly until a loud moan resonated through the wall, and Elizabeth vaulted to subdue it.

He followed her.

Translucent afternoon light settled over the air like shining gauze in moonlight. Silver objects cluttered the otherwise sparse room as if on display in the window of a hospital supply outlet. Pans and bowls carefully molded to catch vomit and urine had been stashed in neat rows under the steel bars of the bed. Tubes and syringes lay dormant on stainless trays, while snakelike rubber hoses hung from tiny cranes, dripping clear liquids into the veinless arm of the skeletal creature swathed in white. He had no hair whatsoever, and his eyes had sunk in like depressions made in bread dough. The lifeless contours of his face revealed a sharpness of bone structure, a square jaw that in health would have made a dynamic impression of character and determination. Lying there against the bleached white of hospital sheets, the facial frame of this man resembled a mass of haunted pick-up sticks grotesquely assembled in a Käthe Kollwitz nightmare.

David helped her lift him, weightless mass of flesh and bone, smothered in bedsores that looked like eyes encrusted with impetigo.

Her husband fell into a soundless doze, and Elizabeth put the bar back up on the side of the bed. David followed her silently into the living room. She turned toward him, her hands folded softly across her chest.

"Don't pity me, and don't bother me. Other than that, I have nothing to say to you except thank you for the journal."

He was paralyzed with tenderness for her, which he dared not conceal.

"You're welcome, Elizabeth. I'm not terribly adept at friendship with women, but if you'd consider it, I could be your friend."

And they had made love, on the floor, by the door, to the moans of the dying, to the clink of metal bars and the raspy breathing of the respirator pumping air into the lifeless lungs in the other room.

They coupled passionately, every day, until all the miracles known to oncology, to medical engineering, and even to God could no longer prolong the life of this useless mass of protoplasm, writhing in agony in the bedroom.

The only loving thing left to do would be to pull the plug on the respirator.

And David helped her to do it.

David made the arrangements for her husband's cremation and sat with her until things were over.

A tender melancholy had crept through what was once a desperate passion, and it seemed to suit both of them better.

They were friends; in fact, Elizabeth was his only friend. His colleagues made little effort to be close to a man who would balk at feeling by ridiculing it with venom, who would humiliate others with sarcastic monologues of self-pity.

Elizabeth had managed to get beyond that with David. Theirs was a friendship born in raw pain, and it would have been redundant to gloss over it with the patina of wearisome games.

Only once had he attempted to push it, to ask her why their relationship wasn't riddled with all the land mines of his other failures.

"It's quite simple. We don't love each other that way, and I don't expect you to give me things you can't."

It was Elizabeth who had suggested he look up his children.

David went to the front office to pick up his message. The clerk reached in the box reserved for room keys and pulled out a pink While You Were Out slip. A phone number was written awkwardly across the top where the name of the person was supposed to be. Sloppy practices irritated David, but he stopped himself from telling this to the elderly gent, who would offer no reasonable explanation.

"Was it a man or a woman?" he asked, annoyed.

"I think it was a girl, but I can't be sure."

Jesus Christ, can't you tell the difference? David thought, but kept it to himself.

"Is there a phone here?"

"You got one in your room."

"I don't want to walk all the way back there. Would you kindly show me a phone so I can decipher this message someone was apparently incapable of recording correctly?"

The old man, seeing David having lost all patience, knew he had pushed some limit that only served to convince him that easterners had no patience or manners.

"Use this one here."

"Thanks." David exhaled loudly and dialed the number.

A woman answered.

"Good afternoon; Pacific Mutual. This is Roger Caldwell's office. How may I help you?"

Many suggestions came to mind, but David dismissed them in the interests of general curiosity.

"Ah, this is David Bartholomew calling."

"Very well, Mr. Bartholomew; what is this regarding, please?"

"I'm sure I don't know; he called me."

"One moment, please."

He was clicked on hold, and before he could protest he was speaking to Roger.

"David, hi. Roger Caldwell here."

"Is something wrong?" inquired David, faintly alarmed.

"No, nothing's wrong. Say, I'd love to talk to you for a few minutes. Could we meet for a drink?"

The cheery nature of his voice distracted David. He could sense no nervous undercurrents of strained innuendos. Perhaps he wished to question him about his insurance needs.

"Well, how 'bout it?"

"Sure, why not?" David could see a thousand why nots, but the tone of the minute seemed to preclude looking for dark shadows.

"What say we meet downtown at the Bonaventure around five. Can you find it?"

"Sure," David replied with confidence, not sure at all.

"See you there."

Terrains of ambivalence, where rules did not matter enough to define, had always held a fascination for David. He did not live in the easy alliance with structure, and yet the casual interplay of relationships in California made him uncomfortable.

You could not break rules where none existed in the first place. First and second spouses played mixed doubles with the former lovers of old wives and husbands. Children of creatively arranged relationships went to Rams games with siblings of sideline unions who were somehow connected to their lives.

Everyone regarded these shifts in pairing with casual tolerance, ironed smooth by the ease of the setting, which seemed to deny dark passions, hidden jealousies, and festering hatreds. It was a general leveling of the sensibilities, where one emotion from the past held little meaning against the pressing promise of the present.

He did not understand it at all.

The shiny black edifice of the hotel rose into the smoggy sky of downtown like a futuristic monolith gently rounded in glass and cement.

He was early. Inside this city within a city, David cruised the flashy shops lit up like vanity mirrors housing expensive clothes and jewelry. Scores of Japanese tourists milled around this spaceship of a hotel in search of what they imagined was L.A. culture.

The escalators and glass elevators charging toward the panoramic bar carried clusters of curiosity seekers, business people hoping for a deal, dandies on expense accounts, and the forever-young crew of hustlers who hung out at the more expensive hotels during the summer, looking for whatever diversion the trade was willing to pay for that season.

David sat in the bar on the top floor and ordered a kir. The view of the city was impressive, certainly not like Boston was, but the sprawling aggression of the buildings had to be admired for courage alone.

"Glad you could make it, David." Roger's hand extended across the table with fierce friendliness. He sat down quickly.

"Coors Light," he signaled to the waitress, who obviously knew him.

"So how's your stay in L.A. so far?"

"Fine." David was thoroughly confused.

"What have you seen to date?"

David ticked off the names of places he'd visited, savoring the irony of sounding like the chamber of commerce.

Roger didn't appear to notice; instead, he offered knowledgeable suggestions of interesting haunts and inexpensive restaurants with ethnic menus.

David studied his face carefully. He decided Roger looked like Jack Nicklaus or Johnny Miller, the same kind of sun-bleached allure that could sell slacks for Sears Roebuck or cars for American Motors.

He talked about Iran's influence on the insurance business. He mentioned a recent Lakers victory, Jason's third-prize ribbon in a surf contest in Santa Monica.

"Sam is doing the sets for an O'Neill revival."

"Sounds interesting," was all David could muster. The man before him was an enigma, a wholesome glob of information concerning people who until only recently had occupied the periphery of David's life.

Roger spoke as if these tidbits should be important to him.

They were not.

Unable to stand it any longer, David leaned forward to interrupt him.

"Roger, why did you ask me to come here?"

He looked stunned, then relieved.

"I wanted to talk to you alone about all this."

"Then talk."

He took one long, deep breath.

"I did not want, or approve of, your coming."

David relaxed. He could deal, at least, with this.

"However, these are your children, though you could hardly be called much of a father. And you were married to my wife, after all. Let me repeat myself. I did not want or approve of your coming here, but I did it for Samantha. She seems to think it's important for the children to have some kind of relationship with you. Personally, I don't think you deserve shit, but I went along with it," Roger said, laying his cards on the table.

"I see," said David. "I appreciate your honesty and your kindness."

"There's nothing kind about it, buddy, from my perspective. I don't like you, but I love Sam and the kids. When you refused to let them take my name, I was furious and hurt. I wanted to kill you. *I* raised those kids, goddamnit, you didn't, and trust me, it wasn't always easy. Rebecca has never been the easiest child."

"Indeed," muttered David.

"I'll tell you a secret. I've always maintained that she inherited her moody, surly temperament from you. Maybe that strikes you funny, but it doesn't me. I love that little girl despite her difficult—at times, impossible—nature. She's a kid who hurts, here, inside, and I have tried to love her despite everything. You may have noticed that she doesn't inspire those feelings in others."

"Yes, I have." David stared at this man with a mixture of awe and confusion.

"And one other thing for the record: I know what you think of my lifestyle and my job. Let me tell you something, Bartholomew, even scholars, poets, and geniuses get sick, grow old, and die. Nobody scoffs at me then, take my word for it."

David sighed again; lucid candor made him anxious.

"So?" David edged, realizing he'd pinned him.

"So, here we are. What can I say?"

"Possibly nothing," David pronounced gingerly. Roger rose to leave and leaned across the table.

"Only this. If you upset Sam or hurt her or us, I will break your fucking face beyond repair."

5

When my father left my mother, I waited by the window, thinking he would come back. I thought they were just mad at each other. I remember them being pissed at each other a lot. They argued and fought and yelled. I thought it was my fault, but now I know it wasn't. They used to say awful things to each other. Jason doesn't remember any of this, but I do. He said she was a frumpy deceiver and she told him he was a selfish dreamer. I never understood those words, but I remember the shouting and my pretty blond mother thinking that everyone in Boylston could hear them.

But the silences were worse. Sometimes the two of them wouldn't speak to each other for days. I thought they hated me. God, I was scared of those silent nights.

One time when David (Dad?) came home for dinner, I reached for his hand and put it into Mom's. They laughed like it was cute, but I was crying and they didn't understand what I was doing.

Jason's too dumb to remember, but I do. I heard my mother say things about Dad to her friend Barbara. I hated it when she called him names and Barbara agreed. He probably chopped her down to someone else.

Then I remember that he just packed up his books and papers and left. And that's when I waited by the window for him to come back.

I cried almost every night. Mom doesn't know that. She cried all the time too, but she doesn't know I know.

I hated her for letting him leave.

She got sick after that and I thought I would become an orphan, like the little match girl. But she got well and we took a lot of walks and the yelling didn't go on anymore.

He never came to see us.

Jason cried all the time. I hated it when he kept us awake. If my dad would come back, I thought, he'd get him to stop. But he never showed up.

I pretended from then. I liked to think that he was coming back and there would be a wedding, and Jason and I would get to come. I made bridal gowns out of Kleenex and put them on Barbie and married her off to Ken. Sometimes Jason would watch or play, but he was too young to understand. Besides, he was too stupid, even then.

I loved these pretend weddings, but I guess I knew that he wouldn't really come back and marry Mom.

I couldn't tell anyone at school, so I didn't. Their mothers didn't let *their* fathers leave. I would lie to my teacher and tell her the reason I was late to school was because my father walked me there every day, and sometimes he was busy in the morning.

I got in trouble a lot then. The school sent me home for socking Tracy Rabinowitz in the face during coloring. I hated her anyway; she was dumb, with her curls and her zipper case full of Magic Markers. I threw things at kids because they all made me sick. Mom was always mad at me then. Jason was her pet. I hated his guts.

He didn't call and he didn't come back. I asked Mom if he was dead, and she laughed.

I didn't think that was funny at all.

Then we moved. Jason screamed all the way to California. He made me sick. The stewardess was nice to Mom about it. I didn't understand why she didn't just slap him.

The first thing I saw in California was the palm trees. I thought they looked like tall, swaying dancers. Maybe my father was here and we were looking for him.

Mom got a job and I hated it because she was never home and I was left in that dump of a house in the Valley with that blimp of a baby-sitter who adored Jason, of course.

School was stupid and so were the kids. I was the best reader and I could cursive-write ages before they could. Nobody liked me there, except the librarian, Miss Hanaford. She gave me books to read, and we'd talk about them afterward. She was nice; I liked her. The kids at school called her Old Maid because she wasn't married.

Who would ever want to get married?

Mom wanted to get married again.

I'll never understand that one.

I remember some of her dates. I thought they were disgusting. They'd come to our house and be real cutesy friendly to us, talking like we were retarded or something. Sometimes they'd ask if we wanted to play jacks or Yahtzee or checkers. God, they were repulsive.

Jason loved them, naturally.

One time this guy named Sidney came around. I could tell he was crazy about my mother. She'd talked to me about him before he came. I thought he was vile. He had a long, twisted kind of face and he talked slowly and deliberately like I was supposed to lip-read or something. He brought Jason and me gifts. Even his presents were stupid. He brought Jason a GI Joe doll, just another reminder of that filthy, disgusting war in Vietnam.

He gave me a doll that peed all over herself, and I was supposed to find her weak bladder charming. He didn't even notice that I had grown up a long time ago and didn't need his pissing plaything.

I called him Sidney the Kidney and threw the doll in the toilet.

That's when we started seeing that doctor who talked to us about our problems. I hated his stupid beard and his ugly Jewish face. Every time we'd go there Mom would cry and he'd keep pulling Kleenex out of a drawer in a bureau by his chair. Why didn't he just put the stupid box on the table?

Sometimes he talked to me and I wanted to puke. I never answered him, except in my mind.

"Tell me about your friends, Rebecca."

What friends, shithead?

"How about school, Rebecca?"

School is stupid, fartface.

"Do you like the beach, Rebecca?"

I think it's purposeless, asshole.

"You miss your father, don't you, Rebecca?"

I cried when he said that.

And then I got mad and the session was over, and when we walked out I slugged some guy in the balls.

It served him right for being there, but I guess he got the last word.

He married my mother.

Roger's okay. He's not my idea of an interesting man, exactly, but he's nice. At first I hated him, but then I didn't, and our life got better when he married my mother.

He likes Jason more.

They all do.

Sometimes when I see them dragging up from the beach together, I want to cry because they look so happy doing something that is essentially pointless.

Both of them are easily amused. I find that kind of disgusting.

I think my mom is happy.

At least she was until that son of a bitch showed up last week.

I watched them watch each other when he came here.

Heavy.

I think they still love each other. Or something like that.

He's smarter than Roger.

I certainly don't love him.

I studied his face when we went out to breakfast.

I look like him, more than I look like my mother.

I probably have his brains; at least I like to read and stuff, unlike my brother, who is hardly a raging intellect.

Mom is somewhere in between.

Roger's different from all of us that way. He went to college and all, but he doesn't seem to like to talk about things you think about.

Like love or pain or beauty.

Maybe he doesn't think them.

I'm sure David does.

He was surprised I read his book. Why do adults think kids are imbeciles? Probably because most kids veg out like Jason.

Well, I don't, and I did read his stupid book, and I meant what I said to him.

He is macho.

I'd like to talk to him about Jane Austen.

He probably won't stay long enough.

I wonder if Mom will see him secretly.

He's not really handsome.

I can see why she loved him once.

Does she still?

I, most emphatically, do not.

As far as I'm concerned, I'm seeing him out of duty (to whom?) and for my mother.

I wonder if Roger's pissed about all of this.

I would be.

Some guy showing up on the scene after all these years. It's like bad B-movie stuff—not that he'd be able to tell the difference.

This love stuff is a waste of time.

I'll never love anyone that much, that's for fucking sure. It's just not worth the energy drain, if you ask me.

I doubt this David will even keep in touch.

He's probably here because he thinks he's old or wants to hustle Mom.

Whatever.

I still see no reason why I have to participate in all this. None of it was my doing.

He's coming back on Sunday.

I wonder what boring pastime he'll cook up this week.

If he takes us to the skateboard park, I swear to God I'll puke.

Jason would love it.

People who don't think much must be happy, because he never thinks and he's always happy, like a demented child.

I'm not happy. Maybe I think too much.

What is love?

Samantha closed the pages of her daughter's journal with guilty uneasiness. She should not have read this. Privacy was an idea she believed in, and tried to live.

She slid aside the bound editions of Brontë on the top of Rebecca's bookcase and slipped the loose-leaf notebook back under *Wuthering Heights.* Tiny explosions of dust danced like fairy glitter in the sun.

This was a gloomy room for a daughter; very few traces of adolescent regalia were anywhere.

The posters on her wall displayed the grotesquerie of Goya and Dali—unlike the walls of Jason's room, which shrieked the exuberance of the latest heavy-metal groups and a collage of ten perfect waves.

Even the bedspread Rebecca has chosen was sad. Chocolate brown tufted cotton dropped in a melancholy heap across the bed.

No scatter pillows, or souvenirs, or knickknacks or cosmetics.

Just books and pencils, piles of writing paper and erasers.

And her journal, solitary keeper of dark secrets and whispered sadness.

She wished she hadn't read it. She hoped David would simply go away. But she knew better. And she knew her daughter was right. At some point, she would see him alone.

6

"Do you have a main squeeze?"

"A what?" David inquired, careful not to take his eyes off the freeway for fear he would miss the turnoff to the Santa Ana Expressway.

"A main squeeze—you know, a primary significant other. 'Girlfriend's' a bit young for you, 'paramour' sounds too romantic, and 'whore' would be rude."

"Shit, Rebecca. Why don't you lighten up on him? If he's got a main squeeze, that's okay by me," Jason assured him.

"I was only asking. Jesus, why's everybody so touchy?" Rebecca whined.

"You'll notice I haven't spoken at all," David said placidly.

"Forget it. We'll all happy up in the Magic Kingdom." She slouched into the bucket seat and opened her book.

Jason leaned forward on David's side. His hot breath

reeked of Hubba Bubba, a sweet and acrid combination of cherry and banana flavors, the remains of which hovered in the corners of his mouth. The fruity fragrance mixed with the rubbery, smelly fog left David feeling nauseated.

Besides, it was barely seven in the morning. Heeding Roger's advice, he'd arranged to pick them up early in order to beat the swarms of summer visitors.

He was hung over; the inside of his mouth felt like cotton smothered in the faint aftertaste of bourbon.

The children had been waiting for him on the steps. Sam and her Roger were noticeably absent. He found that odd, considering.

"Can we ride the Big Thunder Mountain Railroad?"

"I'm sure we can arrange it."

"You know it's a scary ride, don't you?" Jason asked in earnest.

Actually, David knew nothing at all about amusement parks of any kind. The idea of a slab of land being deliberately converted into a series of prefabricated fantasies rather amused him. He'd always found something faintly repulsive about the likes of Walt Disney, who consecrated inordinate amounts of time and energy to a talking rodent with a bow tie. Disney's heavy inclination toward anything connected to the family unit as the sacrosanct kernel of society rendered him suspect and downright creepy. When David had learned of Disney's clandestine bouts of alcoholism, he'd felt oddly relieved; he liked the man a bit more.

"Wanna count the polyester on Main Street?" Rebecca suggested. "Midwest pours in like the harvest this time of year. Listen for how many! 'Doris, don't this just beat all?' or, 'Isn't this cute?' It's revolting."

"Aw, shut up, man, you rip on everything."

"I'm not a man. At least get the gender straight."

"I think the two of you should consider some kind of a tactical truce for today."

"Say what?" Jason demanded.

"He means shut up, that both of us should shut up."

Rebecca resumed reading and sulking by the door. Jason sat and stared at the window. The silence weighed on David. Not that this wasn't preferable to their constant bickering, but it was not a peaceful quiet.

"I didn't mean that no one should talk at all." He kept his eyes glued on the tangled web of freeway lanes, each tributary promising a different direction. Cars raced on either side of him at intolerable speeds. Their impatience with his hesitancy was revealed in the aggressive honking of horns and pantomimed insults. A truck driver blasted him with the air horn of the semi, and gave him the finger in passing. David veered into the right-hand lane, hoping the off-ramp to the Santa Ana Freeway would turn up momentarily.

Factories along the coastline sent up hostile spurts of ebony air.

His children watched his ineptitude at the wheel in stony silence.

"I have no steady companion to speak of," he announced to no one in particular.

Finally, the snow-capped peak of Disneyland's Matterhorn came into view, rising in odd juxtaposition to the purple haze of the morning and the tangle of telephone wires decorating the horizon.

It was already eighty degrees, and according to the forecast would reach ninety by noon.

David drove slowly, careful to follow the clearly marked indications of how to get to the main parking lot. Neon-lit family motels peppered both sides of the road, all of them boasting No Vacancies. At his destination, a sea of station wagons lined up in horizontal symmetry between the bright white slashes of paint on the pavement.

"All right!" shrieked Jason from the backseat, putting his hands on David's shoulder. The hairs on David's back tingled with pleasure. Without thinking, he took one hand off the steering wheel and placed it over his son's.

A little trolley car circled the parking lot, picking up people headed toward the entrance. The three of them jumped on quickly.

Rebecca clutched her book.

"There are two worlds here," snapped Rebecca, "but only one is visible to tourists—unless you make the mistake of looking seedy, unwholesome, or, God forbid, you are smoking a joint or drunk."

She waited for reactions. Jason was so enthralled he didn't hear her. Several passengers clucked at her undisciplined tongue. David was intrigued and only moderately embarrassed by the volume of her voice.

"There is an underground world of dark tunnels leading all over the park. Wandering narcs circulate incognito and snatch the undesirables and whisk them into the bowels of the earth. Sort of Dante's ninth level, run by fascist New Kids on the Block."

"She hates everything."

"Not so. But what I said is true. There is an interesting custom here called the friendly frisk. On grad nights, America's youth are subject to body searches at the gate. Happiest Place on Earth. You saw what the ads say."

David was genuinely captivated by these contradictions. He prided himself on being a person who could always see opposites. In the secret chambers of his pride, he judged that to be his tragic flaw. There was no question that he possessed one; he depended on it.

"How do you know all of this, Rebecca?"

"My friends told me."

Jason tapped David on the elbow. "She doesn't have any friends."

They entered the Magic Kingdom.

Together they strolled up Main Street, past the shops and soda fountains of turn-of-the-century America. Clacking sounds of an old-fashioned trolley commingled with the tinny bounce of a nickelodeon playing inside a penny arcade. Hordes of children clustered around the oversized dancing animals that roamed the sidewalks, grotesquely costumed as cheerful bears and rabbits. Mothers in lime pantsuits and fathers in plaid trousers trotted toward Fantasyland like so many multicolored plovers. There were no papers on the ground, just neatly swept streets peppered with candy-striped trash bins marked PLEASE.

"What are we going to hit first?" Jason asked, in a tone that suggested that he could supply the answer.

"My wish, as they say, is your command." David smiled and returned a half bow, which instantly made him feel foolish, unnecessarily dramatic.

"Good. Then my wish is to go somewhere else."

"Aw, chill out. You ruin everything. Let's go to Tomorrowland. I want to ride Space Mountain."

Rebecca heaved an impatient sigh, but David took her by the arm and escorted her into the land of the future. She declined to ride Space Mountain, so he went on it with Jason, who laughed and yelled at the exhilaration of it all. He fell against his father on the fast curves. David didn't mind at all.

"Your hair's a mess."

"Indeed it is, Rebecca. The wind is brutal up there," he said with mock ferociousness, and took a pocket comb out of his jacket.

"Better?"

"You're all right," she sighed, walking away. He could feel the faint stitches of a headache at the base of his neck. He hurried to catch up with her.

"Look, let's at least attempt to have a decent day. Surely there's something about this place that interests you."

"There is; the exit signs."

"Aw, man, she's such a *drag*."

"Cram it, fag."

"Both of you shut up," he shouted unexpectedly. People stared as they walked by. David cringed with embarrassment. He lowered his voice self-consciously. "I do not want or need this kind of nonsense."

"Then why did you invite us?" Rebecca sneered.

"That's enough of your hostile horseshit!" David snapped.

"All right!" Jason hooted, delighted that his sister was under fire.

"And you be quiet too," he demanded, then studied them both.

"Now, we are going to get in that traveling bucket overhead, move on to the next country, and we are going to have a good time. Is that *clear*!" He was yelling again, his shoulders stiffened in anger. Jason nodded his approval; Rebecca crossed her arms in pouty silence but did not disagree.

They waited in line to board the Skyway to Fantasyland; no one looked at or talked to the other. David scanned the queue of eager faces around him. He dared not peruse those of his own children.

From high above the park one could see the vast expanse of the Magic Kingdom sprawled out like a gigantic game board whose pieces were mobile, colorful, and noisy. The wind blew Rebecca's hair back, accentuating the scowl lines around her mouth. Jason hung over the side, trying to reach out and touch the Matterhorn and spit into the water of the Submarine Voyage.

Rebecca insisted they see the "America the Beautiful" presentation.

"I want you to listen to the hype about the Land of the Free. Do you know I had to take a quiz once on this?"

She was softening a little, and David was relieved. The multidimensional image of the rocky mountains to the oceans white with foam gave him vertigo; the music reminded him of Germanic war marches. Jason spun round and round in order to get a full perspective when they got to Boston.

"Where do you live?" he whispered to his father. David quickly tried to pinpoint a section of the city, but the image switched to the Golden Gate Bridge.

When the lights came on, he could not focus on anything but a bevy of red dots in front of him.

"Well, what did I tell you? I mean, is that a patriotic overdose?"

"Indeed, it appears to be. Whatever was on the test?"

"Names of places and our forefathers."

"No pushing for a point of view?"

"We couldn't say Washington was an asshole, if that's what you mean."

"That is not what I meant at all."

"Forget it."

"Let's ride the teacups," Jason chimed in.

"They give me nausea."

"*Everything* makes you sick." He shoved her in the abdomen.

"Especially you, cretin," and she slapped his shoulder blade.

"Stop, this instant! I cannot possibly cope with the two of you!"

"We knew that a long time ago," Rebecca added, unsolicited. David reached over and grabbed her arm in a fury. His fingers dug into the soft flesh of her bicep. Tears flooded her eyes.

"That's absolutely all of that I'm going to listen to today. I am trying to build something here, and you know perfectly well what I'm saying. I cannot change what happened ten years ago, but I can try to establish something here. I do not need your hatefulness."

She shook her arm free of him and started to sob. Jason had moved to a bench near Sleeping Beauty's Castle. Public fights embarrassed him; in fact, anything to do with his sister did.

He watched her cry as strangers walked by. He could see the pantomime of David's anger turn to gentle scolding, then melt into solicitous joking.

He's probably an all-right guy, Jason thought to himself, but not as nice as my dad.

They made it through the teacups, the Jungle Cruise, the Pirates of the Caribbean, the tree house, and the steamship.

As the sun disappeared behind the crest of Big Thunder Mountain, a heavy fatigue came on all of them, and by mutual consent and no argument, they headed for the car.

Somewhere near the Disneyland City Hall it occurred to him that the purpose of the place was to provide an arena where insufferably perky adolescents could be intent on—no, were commanded to—have a good time. Every trace of ambivalence had been erased by calculated stimulation, mechanical exuberance, neon joy.

This was family entertainment.

He had entertained his family.

7

The sun glistened on the foamy shore-break, sweeping its way up the sand and receding as silently as it arrived.

The paper had predicted perfect beach weather, a July euphemism for horrendous crowds. Dwellers of the inland empires of San Bernardino and beyond would pile in their cars to escape the sweltering stillness of midsummer's heat and head toward promising, salty-cool breezes, scalding sand, and predictably perfect waves. Every foot of sand would be covered in towels of every hue and pattern, one long stretch of wall-to-wall bodies, burning and overexposing themselves to the lure of the Pacific.

Jason and Roger hated them, the pale-faced tourists who scattered litter on the sand, shattered the tranquility of the shore, and ruined all chances of smooth surfing by their intrusive presence in the water.

Roger had phoned in that he would be out in the field

this morning—a frequent white lie when he desired to be elsewhere.

Sometimes he would talk Samantha into doing the same, and as soon as the children were off to school, they would go back to bed, then sneak away to the Bagel Nosh for a fattening breakfast.

He'd wanted her to stay home this morning, but she had a production conference. He'd asked Jason to go surfing instead.

A quiet irritation had settled in Roger's normally calm demeanor. He watched his wife for signs of interest in that son of a bitch from Boston. Samantha gave no clues, no questionable glances or nervous tirades.

She didn't talk about him at all.

That worried him most of all.

"Can I use your wax, Dad? I left mine on the deck."

Roger handed him the paraffin chunk he'd zipped into the pocket of his trunks. Their surfboards lay side by side, two sharklike fins poking up like omens. Jason flipped his board over and began to rub the surface in long, languid strokes. He talked about slashbacks and inside lineups, roller coasters and cross-stepping back to the tail.

Roger was watching a sandpiper pick its way around the sand.

"You didn't hear a word I said. How come you're so bummed?"

"I'm not bummed."

"Then what's wrong? I don't like it when you're quiet."

"Me either. Toss me the wax."

Roger drew short, deep lines on the surface of his board. The paraffin cube shattered in a dozen pieces. He picked up the largest chunk and finished waxing it down. Jason didn't say anything, for fear he'd get mad like he had this morning for no reason. He'd stormed into the family room, turned off the television, sent Jason to his room, and told Rebecca to stay in hers. They hadn't even been fighting.

"Let's paddle out over here. Goddamn tourists are too close in there; they'll cut us off."

The two of them eased over the ripply eddies, paddling like wayward sea lions, careful to lift themselves over the crest before crouching to their knees to build up speed.

Roger's arms moved in graceful strokes, tanned and well muscled from the motions of mobility in the water so carefully rehearsed over the years.

He could feel the steamy scorch of the sun against his buoyant body. The sense of his weightlessness relaxed him. He watched Jason struggle smoothly against the current. His gangly arms moved in a regular rhythm— sharp, strong strokes that sailed him over the pumping sets of waves. He'd learned to do it eagerly, without fear. Roger had made a board for him when he was five. Jason would drag it into the garage and practice hanging ten and crosswalking. Samantha had been so excited about it. She would drag Rebecca, screaming and whining, down to the beach to watch them. Why were all of his memories of Rebecca soundtracked by cries and wails? She'd been so hard to tolerate. Jason had been easy. At first he felt that Samantha mollycoddled her where she should have set limits. It annoyed him to anticipate Rebecca's whiny protests that seemed to accompany their early days of courting. Her tantrums, brought on for no apparent reason, sent waves of anger through him as he watched her mother plead with her for an explanation.

He loved Samantha with a lucidity that frightened him. He could spend his life with her, grow old with her—all the tired clichés he depended on fit and worked—but he wondered if he could tolerate her daughter, and most of the time he imagined he could not.

They had been together for almost six months when the showdown occurred. How carefully he'd rehearsed a speech on how crucial he felt it was for her to crack down on Rebecca. He'd chosen his words, thoughtfully eliminating any inflammatory reference to "spoiled" or "rotten." He'd even planned when to tell her, after the children were safely asleep and they were quietly alone.

He never got the chance. One evening at their apartment in the Valley, Roger suggested they go for a pizza at La Barbara's in Westwood. Samantha rushed to find the children's sweaters, but Rebecca had stuffed hers in the wall heater and refused to go. Samantha pleaded with her to hurry up and get moving, but Rebecca just screamed. The fumes of burning yarn wafted up from the wall heater, and when Roger lunged to yank out the smoldering sweater, it landed on Jason's leg, burning him in three places. Samantha rushed to help Jason, and Rebecca screamed and swung at Roger, hitting him squarely in the ear, causing a carillon of fury bells to vibrate through his head.

And he had completely lost control.

He picked Rebecca up by the shoulders, dragged her into the bedroom, and spanked her until she could scream no more. He threw her on the bed and told her to get in it and shut up before he killed her. As he tore back the covers to show her he meant business, she put her arms around his neck and sobbed like a wounded bird. He let her hug him for a minute, then unraveled her embrace, tucked her in, and warned her to stay put.

Samantha was bandaging Jason's leg with gauze and tape. He cried as much from fear as pain. She didn't dare look at him; he didn't care.

"That goddamn kid's been the boss around here too long."

"And now you're it, Roger?" she asked coldly.

"Listen, that kid is out of control. She runs you around in circles, and you want to find out why. Is his leg okay?"

"He'll be fine. You didn't have to beat her."

"I didn't beat her. I slapped her ass and shoved her in bed, something you should have done ages ago."

"You're no expert, Roger, and she's not your child. Jason, go into the other room."

"You're goddamn right she's not mine! She sure as hell wouldn't act like that at all."

"Well, she's not yours. She's all mine, alone."

She started to cry, but she wouldn't let Roger touch her.

"Look, I do the best I can, Roger. I've been on my own with them for a while. Do you think it's easy? You're so smug. I hate it when you're smug. I have to work and support us, and I have two kids to raise alone. And she's difficult."

He tried to apologize, but she wouldn't hear of it.

"Why don't you just go, Roger. I'll call you in a couple of days."

"Samantha?"

"What?"

"Marry me."

And after much discussion, she did.

They were beyond the kelp beds now, waiting for the swell that would career them to shore. Jason kept looking behind him as if he expected it any minute.

"I hope I don't wipe out like last time."

"I told you, there's a right way to take gas. Just get to the bottom of the wave and kick your board away from you while falling off the back."

"Yeah, I know. You pearled pretty bad last time, but you got out okay, for an old dude."

He likes me better than that other guy, Roger thought contentedly, and waited for the perfect wave.

She stared out the window, wondering if the props she'd ordered for evening had arrived. She needed to track down an old refrigerator—an icebox, actually, like the ones midwesterners used during the Depression. So far she hadn't been able to find one.

Roland, her colleague, had left the office in a huff over a union dispute with the lighting people. Normally a man of icy control and efficiency, he had lately become unstrung over the continuous pressure of special-interest groups capable of stopping a production schedule dead in its tracks. He was a man who felt that all art, and especially that of the theater, should be above such mundane disputes of politics and polemic. The idea of a labor strike infuriated him into a frenzy of despair.

He railed about this to Samantha when he could get her to listen. She was usually too busy to be bothered and would dismiss him with a frantic wave of her hand as she argued with someone else on the phone.

"The show must go on, and they want dental insurance. Eugene O'Neill strangled into silence because of socialized molar control. I can't fucking stand it!"

"They'll settle, Roland, and will make an Olympian effort to get it all together on schedule."

She was too anxious to argue with him on these

issues. Sometimes she enjoyed baiting him, but this afternoon she was eager to be left alone.

She actually didn't much care if the O'Neill revival got off on schedule. Then again, she did. Her work had been her steady friend and companion, and now was no exception. She looked forward to coming into the office, and she always felt excitement at the opening of a play.

Rebecca disturbed her. She'd taken to following Samantha around the house, asking an endless barrage of questions about David.

How did they meet? Where did they fall in love? Did they plan her? Where had they gone to on dates?

Samantha felt compelled to give her answers, although the interrogations inevitably produced ripples of unpleasant souvenirs. She would have liked to talk about it with David. To ask him if he felt Rebecca had the right to know—and if so, how much. Jason didn't ask a thing. But then he probably didn't remember much, either. Rebecca, however, remembered everything, and the memories haunted her.

Samantha wondered if David had a steady girlfriend. It occurred to her he might not be alone in Los Angeles. The thought of him bringing someone with him vaguely infuriated her. Somehow she liked the image of him wandering around Westwood alone, brooding, pensive, and miserable. She fantasized him flirting with a young, adoring waif in Guess jeans and Reeboks who was into health foods and spiritualism. He'd mesmerize her with fancy verbiage, fuck her with desolate frenzy, and drop her with ironic rancor.

She wondered if he'd changed.

The phone rang, interrupting her reveries. It was Roland, shrieking that talks of picket lines were ruminating through the ranks. She reassured him that something would happen in their favor, then hung up.

Almost automatically she picked up the receiver and cradled it in her neck. She thought about it for a while before dialing.

The number came to mind easily. It rang three times before someone answered.

He picked up his own phone.

"Roger Caldwell; may I help you?"

"You could always try."

"I try. What's going down?"

"Us. I'm going to call the kids and tell them we'll be out for dinner. I feel like being alone with you."

"Good, real good. I was beginning to wonder if you wanted to."

"Roger . . . don't."

He sighed heavily. "Okay. Where would you like to go?"

"Pizza and a movie."

"You got it. I'll meet you in Westwood at the Chart House at seven. We'll pick a place from there."

The mention of Westwood set both off on particular nervous tangents.

They simply said good-bye. Samantha looked at her watch. It was nearing 6:30, almost dusk. David had called dusk the hour of sadness, day fading slowly into night.

It was his favorite time to make love, which they would do until the children came.

The dusk became dinnertime.

She wished she hadn't remembered.

Roger awoke in the middle of the night to find the bed empty. He got up to look for Samantha and found her on the couch, staring off into space.

"Hi." He sat down and put his arm around her.

She rested her head on his shoulder.

"He's tearing you up, isn't he?" His voice was calm.

"Not really, but having him here upsets me."

"Do you still have feeling for him?"

"The same kind of feeling I imagine you have when you think about Suzy."

"Suzy's dead."

"Yes, but remember the night you broke down and told me all about her?"

"Yes."

"You told me your remorse would fade, but it would never go away. You kept saying, 'What a waste.' "

"That's different. Was David a waste?"

"Yes and no. I had the children, but I wasted enough time mourning him."

"And now?" He could feel his body grow tense.

"Roger, you and I came together at a very needy time for both of us. In a sense we didn't fall in love, we grew into it."

"Do you still think we're needy?"

"No, he is. We love each other, and I do love you, Roger."

He kissed her gently on the cheek and just held her to him.

"Come to bed, sweetheart," he whispered softly.

I wish he'd stayed in Boston, thought Sam on her way to bed.

8

He'd slept with three different women since he'd been in L.A.; not an impressive record, he thought, all things considered.

He hadn't enjoyed any of them all that much, except for Doris Jean.

His first encounter had been in the library at UCLA, where he spent the week researching Robinson Jeffers. He'd told his colleagues at B.U. that he would bring back biographical information on West Coast poets, a current academic vogue with East Coast intellectuals.

Elizabeth had confided to him that he'd better come back with something, his credibility in the department having deteriorated along with his waning enthusiasm for publishing new material.

A part of him didn't give one holy shit what they

thought, dreary pedagogical boors, all of them; and yet his pride would not allow him to return empty-handed.

David slogged to the stacks and gathered information on the Roan Stallion. And met Cecelia—graduate student, palmist, amateur magician, and asthmatic.

He heard her wheezing over volumes of American literature and watched in horror as she inhaled a mystic potion for a spray bottle that brought the color back to her almost pretty face.

"Are you all right?" he asked, alarmed as the whistle breathing continued to roar up from her chest. She nodded her head yes, since she was holding her breath with the magic medicine trapped inside her lungs.

She exhaled loudly, emitting a pungent perfume of strong medicine into the stale air of the stacks.

"Thanks for asking. I didn't expect that one at all."

He watched the faintest flush return to her cheeks. Her hair was the color of tarnished copper.

"My name's Cecelia, and most of the time I breathe normally in libraries."

"I'm David Bartholomew."

He extended his hand to shake hers. Instead she grabbed it, flipped it over, and looked intently at his lifelines. Slowly and methodically she traced the indentations from their source to their extension.

"You're a hot one, that's for sure. I'll probably fuck you fairly soon. Your love line's too deep to pass up."

And she did. It was something less than earth-moving. Although she was a pretty woman with flaming hair in wonderful places, David could not push aside a paranoid notion that she would lunge into another attack and turn blue under his touch. Every time she heaved and sighed, he braced himself for the death rattle he suspected was right around the corner. It didn't come.

She showed him some card tricks afterward; her sleight-of-hand was almost admirable, but he was scarcely amused.

"I'll like to see you again," she announced, quite naturally.

"I don't allow myself the extravagance of more than once," he lied. "You see, basically I love my wife."

He wasn't at all sure that was a lie, and he supposed on some uneasy level it could possibly be the truth. In any event, she didn't press it, and he never saw her again.

The second lady was more obtuse; he didn't remember her name, and wasn't sure he'd ever asked. He'd picked her up in the bar at the Old World. Both of them, having had too much to drink, sort of slathered their way into bed, both fumbling for a rubber. He found his first.

He assumed that was how it had happened, but he couldn't be sure.

Doris Jean was another matter entirely. Her presence was utterly intrusive. She announced it with crushing finality so that everyone took notice.

"Hi, y'all!" She glistened as she sashayed into the cocktail lounge of the Ginger Man. She circulated and talked to everyone easily, loudly, and personally.

David assumed she was a regular, but his curiosity would not be quieted, so he asked the bartender.

"You must be an out-of-towner if you don't know Doris Jean."

"Correct. Who is she?"

"Doris Jean Sim Jabe is the former Texas Torque Queen, who married the East Indian industrialist who was indicted on seven counts of tax evasion in the last year."

"Never heard of him."

"Had a fondness for drag racing. That's how he met

her. Doris Jean called herself the Princess of the Pits, and I guess it was true. They got married and moved to Beverly Hills."

"Where's he?"

"They have an arrangement," he said, "like most of the people in here."

David pondered that one for a moment, but he was aware of a gush of steamy air somewhere near his neck.

"Are you talkin' about me, sugar?"

Before he could answer, she double-checked it with the bartender.

"He's talkin' about me, ain't he, Clyde?"

And before the bartender could answer, she was back to David.

"Don't make me no never mind, sugar. I'm Doris Jean, the Turbo Queen; the rest is none of your business."

He laughed despite himself and invited her to sit down.

"Thank God; this crowd's about to bore me into a coma. Who or what are you, sugar?"

"I'm David Bartholomew, visiting professor, negligent father, and shameless voyeur. I *was* talking about you."

"Well, I'm a damn sight more interesting than these cadavers in their Gucci-Pucci-Doochie. Hell, you get better stuff back home at TG&Y."

"What sort of stuff?"

"Who cares? Are you married? I am."

"I was married, yes. I am not presently."

"You talk funny."

"So do you."

"Well, touché, I'm gay."

"You are?"

"Certainly not; it's just a rhyme. I'm married. He

don't like to cruise around. I do, so we have an agreement."

"Fair enough."

"No it ain't. I lie to him."

"Oh."

"Look, I like beiges and browns at home, know what I mean?"

"I think so."

"He thinks I like noise and fun, which I do and he don't, but I also crave hot lovin', which I do and he don't."

"I see!"

"Well, he don't, and that's how I like it!"

"Well, you've got that one taken care of."

"I reckon. Why'd you dump your kids?"

"I didn't say I did."

"You called yourself a negligent father. Don't bullshit me, honey; you dumped 'em."

"So I did, Doris Jean. Perhaps it's a question of semantics."

"Whatever blows your skirt up, sugar."

"Do you have children?"

"With Sim Jabe? Honey, that would be a good one. I'm not exactly what you'd call mother material."

"I suppose I wouldn't be considered for a parenting award either."

"Then what did you have 'em for?"

"I didn't."

"Oh, my God, another porko denyin' the part of his pecker. Listen, sugar, let's get out of here and go have some fun before we fight."

"I'm game."

"Figured you was."

"Yes?"

"I ain't fooled by school clothes, dumplin', and I wasn't born yesterday."

"Where to, Doris Jean?"

"Willie Nelson's at the Palomino. He warms me up, if you catch my drift."

He caught it.

She hooted and hollered throughout the show, and when Willie got to "Blue Eyes Cryin' in the Rain" she was sobbing with the rest of the crowd, decked out in jeans and boots and Stetsons. The air was thick with smoke and the pungent haze of burning hemp. Doris Jean carried joints in her bra—three of them—neatly rolled Columbian warmed by the ample bosom protruding from her décolletage, held securely in place by her Playtex underwire. The sensation of being pleasantly high tingled through his body, sending waves of weightless caresses up and down his legs. When Willie sang "The Red-Headed Stranger," he thought about Cecelia and started to laugh. Doris Jean leaned toward him seductively and whispered, "Something musta tickled your tool, sugar, cuz this ain't a funny song."

"I'll tell you later," he lied, and she sat back to join in the chorus of "Amazing Grace." For some reason, the song depressed him, reminded him of days spent in the Old Howard or the Bohemian Café listening to Judy Collins croon the same ballad, except that next to him was Samantha, not Doris Jean, and they had just come from a furtive afternoon of lovemaking and celebrating the hour of sadness in each other's arms. The idea of how long ago that was saddened him.

They had been so happy there.

"You havin' a sinkin' spell, sugar?"

"Caught in the act of nostalgia."

"Bygones ain't never bygones, are they, honey? Wanta blow this joint? I think I'm ready to blow yours."

He would have been lying to himself to say that her eagerness in lovemaking did not excite him into a workable frenzy. She came after him in the car in the parking lot and he let her lustful vigor soothe his sadness with ardent kisses and thirsty moves.

Back at the motel she twisted and turned with blazing zeal, urging and cajoling him to let go and "moan and wail like the coyotes hootin' at the moon, cuz after all, what's left?"

She let him lie on her chest afterward, and they talked of nothing in particular.

"You ain't such a bad guy," she told him before she left. "But you gotta lot of makin' up to do, or else you shoulda' stayed in Boston."

"You're a lovely person, Doris Jean. I've thoroughly enjoyed our evening. You understand a lot."

"Listen, sugar buns," she said, fastening her evening cape, "I said you weren't so bad, but if I'd been your wife, I'da sliced your peter in two if you'da done that to me. See ya."

He'd gone back to the Ginger Man a few days later, but no one knew where she'd gone.

"Why don't you try Daisy's?" the bartender suggested, but he decided against it. Her diagnosis had been correct. He was having a sinking spell, and no relief was in sight except Sunday.

9

"Jason, get your sister and come to the table."

"Aw, man, *Police Academy*'s on. I wanna eat in here."

"Now. No arguments. We are eating at the table tonight. Now go get your sister."

"This is makin' me tired."

"Do what your mother says, Jason, and don't argue."

He whined his way out of the room, and from a distance Samantha could hear Rebecca yelling at her brother to get out of her room.

It didn't matter; they were going to sit down as a family and have a normal dinner. She'd called Roger and told him to be home early so they could have a drink before supper. She'd told Roland to man the office, and she took a long lunch to go grocery shopping.

She drove across town to Farmer's Market to pick

out fresh vegetables and fruit. She planned to make a ratatouille and fruit salad. Roger would barbecue some steaks on the grill. She'd pick those up on the way home from work.

Roland told her she was crazy to do this kind of thing in the oppressive heat of summer.

"It's one thing to slave over a hot stove when it's freezing. I make wonderful stews for Carl during the winter. But in July! I don't care if he starves, and you shouldn't care either."

"I care. Besides, it's good for families to eat together."

"Samantha, please. Aren't you pushing it? I mean, really."

She'd forgotten just how intuitive Roland was. He was the first gay man she'd ever known so well, and despite his biases, he was usually right on target.

Roland hated children, a fact he did not even attempt to hide. He instructed everyone, from maître d's to movie ushers, to seat him as far away from the little savages as humanly possible. He saw all adolescents as neophyte scum awash in a sea of junk food, pimple medicine, unspecific sloppiness, and continuous assaults on grammar.

He had always chosen his lovers carefully, according to two mandatory criteria. They must abhor children and despise any form of organized labor. He'd dropped one paramour when he found a union card in his wallet and a letter from George Meany. He'd had another quick affair with a fellow he'd met on opening night of a Pinter play; when he'd discovered the guy worked as a Big Brother, he'd dropped him too.

"I don't want to be contaminated by the little beasties, even by association."

He did not like Samantha's kids at all. To Roland, Jason's blatant ignorance of all forms of art and beauty appeared tantamount to high treason. And he flat out could not tolerate Rebecca, whom he referred to in private as "that mangy little bitch."

Roland liked Samantha. They had worked well together for years. He liked Roger, too, though he secretly judged his artistic sensibility mediocre. Roger's body, however, Roland rated as sensational.

He thought it was a shame that such a nice couple had to endure such uncivilized larvae in their lives.

The feeling, at least, was mutual. Rebecca and Jason hated him back.

They called him Fruit Loop and worse, when their mother wasn't listening.

It was hard for Roland to cope when Samantha got these gushes of guilt parenting, as he was fond of labeling them.

"I mean, really, Sam, at their age, it's every man for himself."

She took a two-hour lunch that day anyway.

Rebecca carried her book into the kitchen and plopped it on her plate at the table.

"What's for dinner?"

"Ratatouille. Put the book away and get your brother."

"My brother just got me, and I hate ratatouille, and why are we eating together anyway?"

"Don't start in," Roger warned her, taking his place. "Steaks are one minute from done, Sam. Jason! Get to the table! Smells good, sweetheart."

Rebecca rolled her eyes in exasperation. "Sweetheart! What is this, an evening with the Brady Bunch?"

"Aw, shut your face, dog. I'm starving."

"Both of you knock it off."

Roger got up and returned with a platter full of charcoal-broiled porterhouses that he forked onto the plates one by one.

Samantha set the salad and the ratatouille down, surveyed the table for condiments, and, satisfied that everything was all right, sat down.

A nervous silence filled the room spontaneously. Even Jason hesitated before attacking his food.

"We're not gonna say grace, are we?" Rebecca sneered. "I mean, enough is enough. May I have the salt?"

"Of course," said her mother, handing her the shaker. "Saying grace isn't such a crime, is it?"

"Not unless everyone's an atheist, as in this house."

"Speak for yourself, kid," Roger added.

"I want some catsup. Is there any in the fridge?" Jason asked.

"You don't put catsup on perfectly good steak, Jason."

"Since when are you religious?" Rebecca inquired.

"I'm not religious per se, but I'm not an atheist either."

"What's that supposed to mean?"

"More salad, anyone?" Sam interrupted.

"It means that I accept the idea of God, I suppose."

"I don't," said Rebecca. "I think the whole idea's a joke."

"Well, I don't," said Jason. "Most surfers believe in God. It's a feeling you get from the ocean."

"Right. Sunstroke or salt on the brain."

"Aw chill out, scuz bag."

"Stop it, kids."

"Right," Roger mumbled. "You know, Jason does

have a point, Rebecca. Man and nature often connect when they are alone together. I know what he's saying."

"Well, I don't."

"Mellow in; you hate the beach."

"So what?"

"What are you reading, honey?" Samantha asked, anxious to defuse a festering fiasco.

"David Bartholomew's book on the Brontës."

"*Our* David Bartholomew's book?" Jason demanded to know.

"Of course, stupid."

"Where did you get it?" Roger inquired cautiously.

"I checked it out of the library."

"What's it about?"

"Love."

"Oh." Roger sniffed and chuckled. "Is that all?"

"He's got a lot of good examples from *Wuthering Heights* and *Jane Eyre*. He seems to know a lot about it."

"He apparently had a lot more to learn," Roger interjected, surprised at his own pettiness.

"Actually, that book got a lot of attention, Roger. His literary analysis was called brilliant by the critics."

"I wouldn't push it that far," Rebecca added. "Besides, he's not so great."

"I like him," Jason said. "I'm glad he's here. We had a killer time at Disneyland."

"I thought it was disgusting."

"Then why did you cry on the way home, dogface?"

"I didn't cry. I slept. He was too boring."

"Do you think he's boring, Rebecca?" Sam was genuinely curious.

"He's smart, I guess. I like what he said about love."

"What the hell could he have to say about love?" Roger sniffed angrily.

"He had a lot to say, Roger. His chapter on the passion of Cathy and Heathcliff is exquisite," Sam answered explicitly.

"You ought to know," he sniped.

"What the hell is that supposed to mean, Roger?"

"It means he's jealous, if you ask me," Rebecca added.

"No one asked you," Roger yelled. "Why don't you just shut up for once?"

"Rip her up. What a burn," said Jason.

"You shut up too!" Roger shouted. "I'm sick of this goddamn family fighting every time we eat together!"

"We don't ever eat together," Rebecca reminded him.

Roger reached across the table and grabbed her by the shoulder.

"I'm warning you, you little bitch!"

"Don't talk to her that way!" Samantha jumped to her feet. "You can tell her to be quiet, but don't you dare call her names!"

"I'll do whatever the hell I please!" he shouted.

"Why's everybody so mad?" Jason pleaded, starting to cry.

"It's that son of a bitch David Bartholomew," Rebecca hissed. "I told you not to let him come!" she yelled at her mother.

Samantha screamed back, "Don't call your father names, and don't talk back to me! Is that clear?"

Jason was sobbing now.

"I hate this family!"

No one listened.

Roger was screaming at Samantha, who was yelling at Rebecca, who was bellowing at the two of them.

"Why can't we go back and talk about God?" Jason yelled into the feud at the table, but no one heard him.

They were really fighting now. He caught fragments—". . . fuck your love and his passion . . . his daughter's just like him . . ."—and he recalled his mother shrieking things at his stepfather that he wished he hadn't heard.

Roger picked up the bowl of ratatouille and heaved it full force against the stove. A flood of gushing vegetables oozed and splattered across the kitchen, and the shouting intensified.

He wasn't sure whose they were, but he ran from the table in a flurry of hateful sobs and flew out the front door and onto the street.

The blue-black flicker of an old movie on television made incandescent shadows on the wall of his room. He stared at the set without really noticing what was on.

It had been a lonely day for him. Elizabeth had called—returned his call, actually; he had called her. She told him of rumors that his job was resting in a precarious balance.

A jealous colleague had stolen one of his research ideas and submitted it as a proposal for a book that had been accepted. David's own name had been brought up as a possible chairperson for freshman orientation, a solid sign of departmental contempt and a sure indication of a slip in status within the institution.

"How's it going out there?"

"I'm not really sure," he'd told her, in a fit of honest appraisal.

"What are your kids like?"

He had told her as best he could, making sure to include appropriate splices of dialogue where relevant.

"Jesus Christ," was all she could offer by way of comfort or comment.

The call depressed him utterly. He'd gone for a walk in Beverly Hills. Rodeo Drive made him anxiously aware of all he'd never have, even though he found it vulgar and wouldn't want it in the first place.

Wasp-waisted willowy women window-shopped and took no notice of him. He saw several movie stars he judged to be his age, but they looked much younger and were certainly in better shape. The number of wealthy foreigners upset him for no specific reason.

He'd bought Barbara Tuchman's book at Brentano's and went back to the motel to read it, but he fell asleep instead and woke up restless in the early evening.

He soothed himself with Kahlúa and summer reruns. Neither had helped much.

Still he jumped, startled by the sudden knocking, annoyed by the loudness of it.

He tucked in his shirt in case it was Doris Jean, and opened the door cautiously.

Jason stood barefoot and windblown on the doormat. His eyes were red and swollen, and his hair flew off in all directions.

"Hey, dude," he sniffed, "can I come in and talk to you?"

10

Her punishment for calling them immature assholes was to clean up the flash flood of ratatouille. When she tried to protest, Roger threatened her with one month's restriction if she uttered another word.

"Restriction doesn't have much significance to someone who doesn't ever go anywhere," she reminded him.

He told her to shut up.

The shrieks and hollers of the now-accelerated-and-moved-to-the-living-room debacle disgusted her. She could hear her mother hurling insults at Roger, who retaliated with howls of cruel criticism about her, the children, and the prick in Westwood.

It only served to reinforce what she'd always believed.

Adults truly made her sick.

No one even noticed Jason's absence.

She reached for another roll of paper towels to slosh up the remains of the green-and-reddish goo still spattered on all the cabinets, but she paused an instant.

Her mother was crying.

She knew the sounds of those muffled sobs by heart.

Rebecca hated it when Samantha cried. She always felt guilty and oddly responsible.

Roger had lowered his voice to an almost soothing tone. They were talking softer now. She listened carefully to see if they would raise their voices again. Satisfied that this storm had somewhat subsided, she renewed her forced labor.

Adults, she surmised, are a royal pain in the ass.

When she finished and set out for her room, she saw them holding hands on the couch. She stopped to verify if her eyes betrayed her. They had not. Roger and Samantha were on the sofa, whispering remorseful platitudes and holding hands.

"Utterly, completely disgusting," she huffed, and repaired to her room and her books, where love made sense.

She fondled her father's book, a slim but impressive volume. How could one stupid hardback cause so many problems? She opened it to the beginning to verify the copyright, 1979. She was five years old when her father's book was published.

He was still at home then.

She thought about that for a minute.

The dedication was on the next page.

"For S."

Did "S" stand for Samantha? Probably. She would ask her mother. Perhaps the "S" stood for Susan or Sally or Sara, and that's why he left.

The jangle of the phone interrupted her musings. She flew out of her room to answer it.

"I've got it, lovebirds," she bellowed to the french doors leading into the living room.

"Hello."

"Rebecca, is this you?"

"Who wants to know?"

"Rebecca, this is David."

"Ah, the man who came to dinner."

"What?"

"I feel like you've been here all evening."

"Why?"

"Never mind; it's too boring."

"Listen, I need to speak to your mother. It's important."

"She's making out on the couch."

"What?"

"You heard me. They're groping after each other like a couple of middle-aged horn dogs, and it's revolting."

"I need to talk to her. Go and get her."

He added a muted "please."

She announced herself by clearing her throat loudly and obnoxiously like in the movies. Samantha's cheeks were flushed and she was slightly embarrassed.

"What is it, honey?"

"Phone, for you."

"Who is it?"

"David, he says it's important."

"I'll just bet," Roger sizzled, but released his arm so Samantha could get up.

"You hate his guts, don't you?" she asked Roger. He started to get mad, but stopped himself and laughed instead.

"I'm not overly fond of him, no."

"Well, I can't stand him, and you guys force me to be with him."

"That's different."

"I don't think so."

"He's your father."

"Hardly. He gags me."

"Then why do you read his books?"

She didn't have an answer.

"Did you clean up the kitchen?"

"Yes. Do me a favor, next time you regress and have a fit, throw pasta; it doesn't stain."

She left before he could yell at her. She watched her mother speak into the phone. Her face looked alarmed.

"How did he get there? . . . On the freeway? . . . We'll be right down."

Rebecca nudged her mother. Unable to just observe, she wanted to know what was going on. Samantha told David to hold.

"It's okay, Rebecca; no one's hurt. Jason hitchhiked to his motel."

"What for?"

"He was upset. He's there with his father. Now go away and let me talk."

Rebecca stayed right where she was.

"Sam," David said, "why don't you let Jason spend the night. I'll bring him back in the morning."

"I don't know, David. This is getting pretty crazy."

"So I understand."

"What does that mean?"

"Look, I didn't mean to upset everyone."

"You haven't upset everyone."

"*Enfin*. He's here. No shoes, no money, no jacket. This will give me a chance to chat with him. There's plenty of room. I'll even buy him a toothbrush."

"He has a toothbrush."

"Not here."

There was a silence for a second, until David shattered it.

"Would you like to talk to Jason?"

"Yes. Put him on, please."

"Hi, Mom."

"Jason, what are you doing?"

"Nothing."

"Are you okay?"

"Yeah. I hate tonight."

"Me too. Do you want to stay there?"

"Yeah."

"Okay then. You be good. He'll bring you home in the morning."

"Okay."

"Jason?"

"Yeah?"

"I'm sorry about what happened. These things are difficult for all of us."

"It's a bummer."

"I love you."

"You wanta talk to him?"

"No. See you tomorrow."

She hung up slowly and ran her hands through her hair. She always smoothed her mane when her life was ruffled. The children teased her constantly about it.

"Why are you talking to him about toothbrushes?" Rebecca demanded.

"Toothbrushes?"

"You said, 'He has a toothbrush.' Everyone has a toothbrush unless they're disgusting."

"Jason's going to stay the night with his father. He wants to talk to him."

"Jesus, who'd ever want to talk to him? Who'd ever want to talk to Jason? Maybe it's perfect. Two losers can talk to each other."

"Stop it. This kind of turmoil makes me weary."

"I didn't start it."

"I know."

"Roger's really jealous, isn't he?"

"Not really. This is hard for him. My life with your father has nothing to do with our life now."

"Mom."

"Mm?"

"Do you love him?"

"Who?"

"David."

"I did, Rebecca. I loved him very much. I do not love him now. Can you understand that?"

"I don't understand loving any man. I think they're all a pain in the ass."

"You will, sweetie."

"Will what?"

"You'll love somebody. It's a very special feeling, Rebecca, and it's a wonderful one. It's just that sometimes it doesn't stay that way."

"Do you love Roger?"

"Yes, Rebecca, I do, a lot."

"As much as you loved David?"

"It's a different kind of love. When I loved your father I was very young, Rebecca, and I didn't know a lot about things."

"What kind of 'things'?"

"Things that make sense."

"Nothing makes sense."

"Rebecca, when I was first with your father I loved

crazy things, like the color of his eyes, the way he laughed. I loved the way he *smoked*. I don't even *allow* people to smoke around me now. Do you understand what I'm saying?"

"Do you love Roger's eyes and how he laughs?"

"Yes, but I love other things more. I love that he loves us and takes care of us, and we take care of him. I love it that he stays when things get awful because he believes things will get better, and they usually do. I love that he likes to come home to us and that he believes in love even though most of the time it's a mess."

"Doesn't David believe in love? He writes about it."

"Honey, I don't know what he believes in now. I think he tried to love us all in his way. His way didn't work out."

"Then why has he come sucking around us now?"

"Because I think he'd like to find a way with you kids."

"How come men get to take up so much of your time floundering around?"

She kissed her daughter, and Roger walked into the hall.

"The couch is empty. Where are you? What did Iago want?"

"Jason's with him. He hitchhiked down to Westwood to talk to his father. He's spending the night."

"Over my dead body!" Roger yelled, out of nowhere.

"Roger, don't be silly," Samantha argued.

And they were fighting again. Shrieking and hollering like violent gusts of the changing Santa Anas.

Rebecca stormed back to her room and slammed the door.

Adults, she figured, are a maladjusted group on just

about all levels, and as far as she was concerned they all made her stomach acid drip.

She sat on the bed and tried to imagine who "S" could possibly be.

11

"What do you say we walk over to Swenson's for an ice cream?"

"Righteous."

"If you say so."

David chose to ignore the bare feet and scruffy hair, although on the way over he kept an eye out for lighted cigarettes or broken glass on the sidewalk.

Jason was small for his age. David noticed the skinny stamens of his tanned and bruised legs hanging out from under his atrocious shorts with the baggy legs. He was a cute boy, David thought. He looks like his mother.

"Would you like to tell me what happened there tonight?"

A part of him was eager for every lurid, juicy detail. He took a certain pleasure in having disrupted the seemingly calm exterior of their cozy family unit. Still, the boy's distress upset him. He had not anticipated that emotion and felt a surge of tenderness toward this scruffy runt.

"You probably shouldn't of come around here. Everybody's pretty mad about it."

"Who's mad?"

"Well, Rebecca's mad—but don't get uptight over that scuz, cuz she hates everybody. Still, she pissed off my mom and dad because she yells so much when we have to see you. Then she reads your books. That's what started the fight tonight."

"What book?" his vanity piqued, he was somewhat ashamed to push it but asked anyway.

"The love book about the Bronsons."

"Ah, that one."

"My father doesn't think you know shit about it."

"The Brontës?" He was genuinely shocked by this revelation.

"No, man, love. My dad thinks you're a son of a bitch—he said that, not me. Anyways, I don't think he likes it that you're here."

"Apparently not. To say the least." David pondered Roger's threat.

"Well, he gets pissed at my mom. He's always mad at Rebecca, so that doesn't count, but I don't like it when he gets mad at Mom. He's a cool dude, you know."

"I'm sure he is."

"For sure he is. We do everything together. You should see him take a tube. He can blast his way to the shoulder and cut loose down into the hook and take it in. The guy's a killer."

"He sounds most admirable."

"Well, he's all grumpy since you're here, and it's not much fun to hang around him, know what I mean?"

"I think so."

"My mom's all weirded out too."

He would have liked Jason to elaborate further, but they were walking by the Wherehouse, and the resonant blasts of a wailing coterie of punk singers filtered into the street and enraptured his son within seconds.

Jason ogled a window display of childlike mannequins all dressed up in jeans and sneakers, who were holding an album featuring a photo of four unkempt-looking deadbeats. Their haircuts reminded him of the hack jobs done on novitiate nuns he'd observed in films starring Audrey Hepburn, where some sadist took pinking shears to her lovely tresses, after which she took the vows.

"Don't you think they're *hot?*" Jason inquired.

"Utterly."

"How about Young M.C.'s 'Bust a Move'? It's killer."

"I suppose I don't know them."

"Do you like Poison?"

He shrugged his shoulders.

"Metallica?"

"That's a group?"

"Aw, man, get with the program. Don't you like music? I like Thrash and Speed Metal."

"Well, yes, I do."

"What kind, dentist office stuff?"

"No; mostly I enjoy classical, although some of my albums might surprise you."

"Such as?"

"The Beach Boys."

"They're gay."

"They are?"

"Their music's gay faggy sickening, even if they did sing about surfing. They're still gross."

"How about Bob Dylan?"

"I don't get off on his songs."

"He used to sing about things that were really important to us."

"Really? Well, that must of been a long time ago."

"So indeed it was, Jason."

"Mom probably listens to the kind of stuff you like. She's all grumpy lately, too. I think you should of just wrote us."

David resisted the urge to correct his grammar and ushered him inside Swenson's. A perky blonde with a wide smile told them to take a number and she'd be with them in turn.

Jason squinted to read the choices. His lips mouthed the words as they scanned the redwood board listing all the flavors in alphabetical order. David studied the cluster of people lined up for cones.

He surmised that the young ones in jeans and T-shirts were students at UCLA. Apparently the sportif look was the latest foil against aging, since he was surrounded by chic forty-year-olds in designer warmups that looked like paratrooper gear. He could decipher no signs of sweat or strenuous exercise. Most of their expensive running shoes looked as unmarked as their wrinkle-free tanned faces. The women looked hipless and svelte, as if their bodies had been carved from ice shavings of a master caterer. Most of the men carried satchels tastefully designed to look masculine and businesslike.

He could smell the mélange of aftershaves wafting around the fumes of flavored ice cream.

She called their number.

"I'll have a double scoop of bubble gum on a sugar cone."

In horror, David watched the fair-haired girl in the

brown checkered uniform scoop up a ball of pastel pink mush peppered with royal blue dots whose dye ran like azure teardrops onto the rosy surface. She scooped out another round ball, plopped it on the first, then handed it to Jason.

"What will you have, sir?"

Sir.

His new appellation by anyone under twenty-five. The very mention depressed him—and surprised him a little—each time it was addressed to him.

"One scoop of chocolate, please."

"Wanna bite?" Jason offered, holding out his melting treasure.

"No thanks."

"It's bitchin'. You should taste it."

"Pass."

David forced himself to smile while he watched in detached disgust as Jason sucked out each blue chunk and proceeded to chew them one by one into a gigantic ball of bubble gum. Layers of pink frost oozed from the corners of his mouth. David turned away to eye the beautiful people instead.

Jason ate with relish, savoring every lick with a loud and succulent slurp.

He washed his face in the drinking fountain afterward.

David pretended not to notice. Jason dried his face off on his sleeve.

"Wanna cruise around?"

"You mean walk a little? Sure, I'd love to. We'll head over on Le Conte and turn down Gayley."

"Whatever. I like not having my sister along."

"Me too," he whispered cautiously.

"Did you leave because of her? I could dig it if you did."

"No, I did not leave because of her. I was not a happy person when I left, Jason."

"Are you now?"

"More than I was then, yes. You see, it's hard to explain, but sometimes things overwhelm people, become more than they can deal with."

"You mean we totally ozoned you out and you couldn't handle it."

"Something like that, yes."

"When things get too heavy for me, man, I just go to the beach and get cosmic in the waves."

"It's not quite so simple when you're older."

It occurred to David that it was not altogether unpleasant to walk along conversing with this sea urchin without shoes. No one stared at them like they were mismatched or unnatural as a pair. He assumed people surmised them to be what they in fact were. A father and son out for a walk.

"How come you came back?"

"I wanted to get to know you."

"But you knew us once and boogied on us."

"Yes, I did. As I said, Jason, I was not a very happy person then."

"Sounds like you were totally screwed up, if you want my opinion. I mean, that's a pretty rank thing to do."

"I agree. But here I am, and I'm sort of hoping for a second chance."

"You've sure done a number on everyone."

"I haven't meant to."

Jason studied his father's face intently. It was traceless, except for the nervous flicker of an eyelid that twitched when he was nervous or overly tired.

"I hope you're not gonna screw up my family, know what I mean?"

"I think I do." He knew exactly what the boy meant.

"Since you've been here, everyone's ripping everyone else. Except for Rebecca, who burns anyone."

He could think of nothing to offer the boy by way of reassurance except that he would be leaving in two weeks and things would return to normal.

Jason got quiet after that.

"Let's go back to the motel and watch TV."

"Is there something special you'd like to see?"

"What's tonight?"

"Wednesday."

"Radical killer night! "Unsolved Mysteries." Let's go."

Apparently his child could give an annotated recitation on the *TV Guide*'s summer lineup. He did not know whether to be impressed or appalled.

They raced each other back to the motel. Jason won by several lengths.

He flipped on the television, found the right channel, and complained loudly that there was no cable hookup. He made himself comfortable on the queen-size bed. The bottoms of his feet were black from the dirt and soot of the streets. He continued to pop the now-faded blue bubble gum in loud cracks.

David studied him throughout "Growing Pains" and "Head of the Class"; he wanted to understand precisely why Jason would be mesmerized by such pap, what exactly he found amusing. He also wondered if he could in fact decode the absurdity of the stories.

He waited patiently until the last commercial. Jason bolted up for a critique.

"Wasn't that totally insane?"

"Yes."

He decided to just watch the next ones with him—go with the flow, as his students would chide him.

Jason sat closer to him during "Jake and the Fatman," and by the time the anchor gave the news update, he was asleep in David's arms. And for the first time in years, he felt tears welling up in his eyes. He did not stop them from falling.

 **12** "Roland, my life really stinks."

"That's a given, petal. Anyone who breeds has a putrid existence."

"Stop it; you don't, and your life is frequently terrible."

"That's because I'm a victim of love."

"Is that what you call it? The furniture for *Iceman* has not arrived, by the way."

"Fucking teamsters, I suppose; they're transporting it and have decided the overtime's not enough for a vacation on Maui. Dogs, all of them. What's really on your mind, pet?"

"I let him come back because I felt I owed it to the kids."

"Lies! Lies! Ophelia! Why don't you simply call him, love?"

"For what?"

"To find the flaw, precious; then you can get *on* with it."

"I know his flaws, Roland. I think I've become reacquainted with all of them, and I still hate them. Besides, I love Roger."

"Of *course* you love Roger, lamb chop. That's not the point. You're talking about a cure for a nagging sore—there, there's your flaw; he's a nagging, festering boil. Call him."

"I don't know what I have to say to him, except Go away."

"Love bunny, listen to Roland. *Naturally* you want him to go away as much as you want him to stay here and writhe with suffering. Personally, I would play this one out to the final curtain, but then I've always been a sucker for tragic love."

He sighed languidly and reviewed his private arsenal of bittersweet encounters. There had been several that had threatened to break his heart. Somehow he'd always managed to pick up the scattered souvenirs and move on. Carl frequently pointed out that Roland set himself up for disillusionment. "You fling yourself at some worthless beauty and poof, you're ready to give up all your real talents and run off with trash."

He was right. Time after time Roland had lost his head over some mindless boy—lent him money, given him gifts, found him a job, or introduced him around—only to be dropped and ignored, devastated and depressed. Most of the time Carl was there to help him reassemble the pieces. Roland depended on that and loved him for it.

"How is Roger holding up here?"

"He doesn't like him at all. Neither do the kids. Neither do I."

"God, it's all there, isn't it, angel? Have you noticed that even in the theater the shits get center stage? Amanda gets to piss around about Tom, Iago flails Othello, Lady Macbeth swells up to her full forty, George and Martha get to devour perfectly innocent people, and we *listen* to them, we *believe* them, we *pay money* to try and understand them! I can't fucking stand it!"

"Me either."

"Call him," he said. "For all our sakes."

She had already decided that she would.

He tried to recall his son as a baby, but no solid image would come to mind. Jason had been the easy baby, but in comparison with Rebecca any child would have been less troublesome.

He remembered when Sam told him she was pregnant. The tightness in his chest had never left him. He pleaded with her not to go through with it. Looking back, even now, he failed to see that as an unreasonable request. A terrible sensation of dread had overcome him. They had no money. Their apartment, a dank, depressing walk-up in Boylston, would never do for a baby. He needed to establish himself by publishing more and lecturing to adoring freshmen that Milton and Donne were as essential to living as air and water.

Part of him believed that was true, but more of him loved Samantha with an intensity that made him shudder.

He fancied her his graceful Griselda, his gentle Guinevere, all lithe and allegro, full of lofty notions of art and beauty and dedicated to pursuing love as an irresistible calling.

He had never known anyone like her before. The undercurrent of sadness that ran through this woman only served to drive him into a frenzy of relentless passion.

When she told him the details of her mother's suicide, he had cried and she hadn't.

When he had met Samantha, he had told her he had no family except Nellie, which was essentially more true than not.

And he had loved her instantly. She worshiped all that was fine and cultured and good. She neither dressed nor acted like the other Mount Holyoke girls, who droned on about economic systems, pathetic fallacies, feminism, breast-feeding, and nuclear waste. She cried at the beauty of a Delacroix, was moved by the poignancy of Poussin, and he could not help but love her. He had begged her to stay with him forever.

He could not recall ever being so happy. At odd hours of the day or night he would freeze-frame her in his memory and remind himself that he was still David Bartholomew and that she, blond and beautiful Samantha, was his wife and his life.

He could not abide the intrusion of another person.

Not even a baby.

So carefully had he built this reality that the idea of an accident distorting the calm was unthinkable, even ominous.

"We'll have it taken care of, Sam."

"I don't want it taken care of."

"You can't be serious."

And of course she was, and she won.

Or lost.

He watched her belly grow with a large swell, and he despaired. She would talk of plans of this pram or that crib, and he would shiver with trepidation and turn morose and hateful and distant.

He remembered lying next to her, drawing her close to him as was his habit and his desire, and the lump of her swollen flesh lay between them like a stubborn stone that would not be lifted. When he moved himself closer to her, he could feel the jabs of the baby's kicks against his stomach, and his heart would stop and his mouth would turn dry, and he wanted to sob to her that he could not possibly bear this unwelcome mass, growing like malignant cells run amok in the skin of his love.

And the baby kicked and moved, and he grew silent.

He felt this was his punishment for such selfish, awful thoughts, and indeed Rebecca did not disappoint him.

Sam's water broke as they were making love. A flood of warm liquid soaked him thoroughly and took him off guard. His golden princess writhed and screamed for thirty-six hours before Rebecca, willful and capricious, squirmed her way out of her mother and into the world that she would forevermore see as hostile.

She was an impossibly demanding child—hungry, cold, or wet, and beyond. She would not tolerate being ignored or shut out. Her cries pierced the wall of the apartment, drove her mother ragged, and lanced David's heart with the predictable pain they carried.

He could not bear to watch Samantha nurse her. This dark-haired infant would suckle loudly and greedily, as if to remind those present of her place in the household.

She grew strong and healthy, and with each new phase came a new set of demands imposed on them as edicts.

She followed David everywhere around the apartment, a precocious talker constantly demanding to know "What this?" When he would hug Samantha, which was rare at the time, Rebecca would race across the floor and sink her teeth into his leg, with a discordant No! before her assault.

She cried all night, demanding books, water, toys, attention.

David begged Sam to leave her one summer and come with him to Europe, where he'd been awarded a sabbatical.

"I can't leave her, David. You don't leave a child."

He had pleaded and cajoled, bribing her with promises of moonlight gondola rides under the Bridge of Sighs, a walk in the Alps, serenades in Granada, sonatas in Salzburg.

He wouldn't hear of bringing the baby.

She wouldn't hear of leaving her.

So, in essence, they left each other; and they fought and screamed into each other's deaf ears until Jason was created in a restful interlude, and their lives were firmly severed for good.

He could remember, with astonishing clarity, the twisted, tormented visage of Rebecca at the window, waiting for his arrival, though it would scarcely change her mood. She smelled of tears and sadness.

Of the child who was easy and loved him, he had no recollections at all.

13 ❧ ❧ ❧

Rebecca crept into the family room cautiously. She'd planned her moves carefully. Her parents would be out until about eleven. If she approached him with treats and moderate enthusiasm, he'd talk without being overly suspicious. She'd catch him somewhere between "Jeopardy" and "Win, Lose, or Draw."

She made brownies and poured two glasses of milk, making sure they were exactly even.

They jiggled like liquid snow as she approached the television area with the tray precariously balanced in her grip.

Jason didn't look up; his body lay supine on the floor, spread out like a lilting jelllyfish, with pillows stuffed under his neck for lazy viewing of prime-time entertainment.

"Want some?"

"What?" he belched out, not taking his eyes off the set where Cal Worthington was espousing the virtues of driving a bargain beetle, while sitting atop his dog Spot—in this case, an elephant. Rebecca caught him smack in the midst of his jungle boogie.

"I made some brownies."

"Why?"

"Because I felt like it—Jesus. Do you want some or not?"

"They got any magic herbs in 'em?"

"Don't be revolting. I don't pollute my system with artificial stimulants."

"Aw, man, you're *such* a drag. Have you ever had a cosmic brownie?"

"I wouldn't tell you if I had."

"No, see, you don't even know what it's like to be fryin'."

"And you do? You're so full of it, Jas."

Jason had stuffed an entire square into his mouth, which he opened slightly to exhale some of the steam of the oven trapped inside the dough. The chocolate cavern reminded her of mud slides in rainy season.

In the background some whiny pubescent boy was arguing with his parents over the merit of gel versus paste for his orthodontically perfect teeth.

"Good," he mumbled, grabbing another brownie and reaching with his other hand for the milk.

"Sometimes I like to fix stuff like this. You're the only one who'll eat it. Everyone's always on a diet around here."

He gave her a curious stare. She didn't talk like this, much less to him. She smiled at him; he was assailed with confusion.

"What's the matter with you?" he muttered, wiping an earth-colored smudge on his sleeve.

"Nothing. I just thought it would be nice to have a treat and watch television. What's on now?"

"Cosby."

And he slunk back into his pillow to stare at Bill Cosby trying to relate to his teenage daughter. Jason thought she was cool, unlike his own scuzzy sister, who was acting weird as usual.

"I'll watch it with you," Rebecca chirped, settling into the shag rug next to her brother, who was solidly uncomfortable with his new persona. He braced himself for her barb of sarcasm, some cutting jab about how stupid everything in the world was, or at the very least he wondered if she would unexpectedly sock him. He eyed her suspiciously, but he could detect no glint of warfare on the horizon.

By the next commercial he allowed himself to relax a little, and toward the end, when MacDonald's was reassuring the American public that the happiness of the nuclear family was safe and sound within the soft folds of a hamburger bun, he helped himself to another brownie and told her they were pretty cosmic anyway.

She allowed herself to become absorbed into the flicker of the prism of colors. The dancing dots she saw instead of the picture made her dizzy. The noise assaulted her ears. She silently counted how many times the show's main message could be repeated lest the audience miss its dopey platitude.

At last check, it was five, before and after the commercial breaks, which were even more ridiculous than the show.

She had never trusted a Mattel-it's-swell toy to make her happy, nor had she ever believed that longing sprays of Le Jardin would bring her popularity and friends. Those kinds of pap promises only made her more hateful, reinforced the notion that most adults lied to begin with in telling you that the world didn't stink.

She knew better.

His breathing was shallow and rhythmic, except when he laughed, which was frequently, although for the life of her she could not figure out why.

"Jason?"

"Mm?" His eyes remained glued to the set.

"What's David like, really?"

"He's a cool dude." And Jason went back to watching TV. She waited a full fifteen minutes before asking, "Did he say anything about me?"

Roger held her hand through the last half hour of the video of *Apocalypse Now*. It was one of his favorites, and Samantha consented to see it again. The tension between them was dissipated by the anxious foreboding of the film.

Martin Sheen made his way up the river, getting closer and closer to Captain Kurtz.

Roger had never read *Heart of Darkness*; the name was lost on him.

In the beginning he had supported Vietnam. He'd even investigated enlisting, but was disqualified because of his allergies. The very notion of communism scandalized him. He firmly supported the free enterprise system and labeled any governmental control an undermining force to democracy. He was the boy raised on films of red scourges and communist hordes, and though he no longer accepted these facile, black-and-white concepts, in his heart he always felt that the true horror of Vietnam was that we hadn't won.

Samantha closed her eyes to the heads strewn about the smoldering sands of the jungle temple. Roland had warned her about that scene; he was in the habit of giving blow-by-blow descriptions of any film he and Carl saw and liked.

"Just wait until you get a gander at Brando, dumpling; he's let himself go to *seed*. Fat as a wallering sow, and bald to boot."

Ominous drumbeats announced the approach. She squinted for a second to verify where Martin Sheen had gotten, and quickly chose the darkness.

Samantha had never been for that dreadful war. David had schooled her in the horrors of napalm, the boorishness of General Westmoreland, and the crimes of Lieutenant Calley. She'd joined knots of East Coast intellectuals and university types in letting her opinions be known.

She had mainly believed they would make a difference.

"We march for causes other than ourselves," she'd yelled at David in the midst of a festering, aching fight. He'd accused her of being mundane and selfish, shortsighted and small.

Yes, yes, she had wanted to say to him. I'm all of those and worse. Can't you just love me?

But she had kept silent, at his side, marching, picketing, protesting. Pouring passion into causes that left them safely unmoved.

And she had been grateful for the time together, for being included, for him not retreating to his books or his classes, his women.

Thinking back on it now, her stomach tightened in anger. She squeezed Roger's palm, and to reassure her that this was, after all, only a movie, he squeezed back.

Brando looked like a grotesquely bulimic Buddha, all self-important and serious.

Roger was enraptured by his speech to Martin Sheen.

She remembered what he'd gotten paid for those few minutes on the screen. Roland kept track of such details.

She figured that he must be an insufferable man to live with, though she had no information except tabloid gossip.

An unspecific hostility was festering within her. She thought back about David.

He'd come home early one day, which was odd, because at that point his homecomings were sporadic and sullen and awful.

Some romantic coed, awash in the idealism of social protest, had brought him a MOTHERS AGAINST THE WAR bumper sticker.

For whatever convoluted reason, it had struck a wickedly funny chord in him, and he had taken the subway home to share his mirth.

Samantha had not been amused. She read the statistics daily—the casualty lists, as journalism so guardedly labeled them.

It was 1979 and the mothers' group was still around. She'd seen them on TV and sympathized with their cause. David's sarcasm bridled her.

To her a death was a death.

And for every boy who died, she knew there was a mother out there who grieved in a way no other person would ever grieve. She felt a connection to those women, an unspoken bond that, yes, she too was a mother, and the thought of someone stealing her child's life was unthinkable, treason, murder.

She knew that beside every ebony body-bag was a mother's mourning and a mother's fury so fiercely mixed with a love no man and his war games could ever understand that it was futile to discuss it, except to tell them in homilies that war is not healthy for children and other living things.

No, she was not amused at all.

Rebecca had become unglued by the screams and shouts of that fight. She'd raced into her infant brother's room and shoved over his crib. The resounding thud stunned them both into a truce, as they pushed each other aside to get to the bedroom.

Jason lay sleeping, undisturbed on the sloping mattress that had slid out from the force of the fall. He'd rolled precariously close to the edge, but the motion had not awakened him.

His odd restfulness quieted them, humbled them for a minute.

They examined him carefully; he was unharmed, and they both felt a little ashamed.

Rebecca stood in the corner and shivered, not sorry for what she'd done but scared of reprisals.

Sam thought that would soften him, calm him, encourage him to be real and authentic and loving.

But he started in again, following her back into the living room, goading her about being a Peace Mother.

She slapped him across the face, and he left for three days.

The old, familiar pain welled up in her again.

She opened her eyes in time to see Martin Sheen lower the blade to Brando's skull and hack him into bloody pieces.

Good, she thought to herself. In the movies, at least a bastard gets what he deserves.

14

A scrim of tension fell between them as soon as she opened the door. His carefully rehearsed casualness evaporated into a stiff formality tinged with nervous irony.

"You're looking chipper today, Sam."

She made no comment but ushered him into the front room. Her hair was yanked back into a ponytail secured by a piece of colorful yarn. Large sheets of white paper lay like opaque windows on the rug.

"The children will be ready in a second, David."

She did not elaborate further or accord any warmth to her voice. Instead, she flopped back down on the floor, Indian style, reached for a black felt-tipped pen, and began to scrawl deep gashes on the blank sheet in front of her. She felt a strong urge to tell him to get the hell back to Boston, where he belonged.

"What's that?" he asked politely, his tone inferring that he understood he was supposed to pose that question.

"My work," she said tartly, and resumed drawing.

"Oh," he mumbled, noting that her anger caused the faintest flush to come to her cheeks.

He remembered that from before.

"Where's Roger?" he pressed.

"Out," was all she offered. Her terseness goaded him to become more cheerful and expansive.

"I've planned a picnic in MacArthur Park for today. I thought we'd mosey on down there, as they say here in the West, somewhere around noon. Afterward I thought a swing through the museum and the tar pits would elevate us, so to speak."

"You mean we get to eat tuna sandwiches with the muggers? How boring."

Rebecca.

She slung her backpack on the sofa, crossed her arms, and leaned against a credenza.

"Do you have any clue as to how dangerous that park has become? Gang wars, murders, mutilation, muggings? You probably picked it so you'd feel at home."

"Hey dude," Jason chimed from behind. David could smell the peanut butter on his breath. "What's the word for today, bro?"

"The word is boring," Rebecca sneered.

"Aw, man, does she have to come? Where we goin'?"

"I thought we'd have a picnic in the park, to begin with."

"Oh, that's insane. I'll get my Frisbee."

"By all means, Jason," David agreed.

"Oh, God, this is beginning to sound like a Pepsi commercial. Mom, do I have to go?"

David waited tensely for her answer. On the one hand he would have liked for Samantha to lash out at this rude child, and yet he would have been totally averse to Rebecca staying home.

"Rebecca," Sam stated matter-of-factly, "don't."

Samantha would give him nothing at all today. When Jason returned with his gear, she made no attempt to get up.

"Have a good day, kids. What time will you bring them back, David?"

He matched her politeness.

"What time would be good for you?"

"When they're ready to come home, I guess."

"I'm ready now," Rebecca snapped, then added, "Let's move this circus to another town."

He closed the door with a soft, resounding thud. He had not looked back to say good-bye.

Son of a bitch, Sam thought, and went back to her designs.

The park had filled early, despite the exhaust fumes and smog and the blistering sunshine the weatherman had predicted would only intensify.

Scores of families had already staked their territory with bright blankets, children's toys, and Styrofoam hampers. Clusters of Chicano men in sleeveless T-shirts played soccer on the charred lawn. The clacking sounds of Spanish wafted in the air like singing castanets. Under the immobile eucalyptus trees, Mexican women huddled together feeding small children and laughing in loud soprano spurts. Orientals roamed, leading young children near the polluted water of the lake to sail small vessels made from balsa wood.

There were vagrants and clergy, young mothers and infants, cruising teenagers looking for action, and the usual coterie of old folks scattered about the benches like discarded humanity.

"How 'bout here, kids?"

"One place is as bad as the next. At least it's shady."

"Shut up, scuz. This is cool. We can throw the Frisbee here."

"Very well."

He spread out the purloined top sheet from his motel and set down the bags of groceries he'd bought at the market on the way to pick up the kids. It had amused him to shop at a store called Lucky.

The irony soothed him as he made his way up the aisles of packaged macaroni, bottled salad dressings, and canned vegetables. At home he had things delivered or ate out. Pushing the silver chariot around on the linoleum struck him as oddly anachronistic. The background music played themes from *Love Story* and *Dr. Zhivago*.

The shoppers hummed along with these familiar tunes. The frisky part of him wanted to halt and lecture to them loudly on the ludicrousness of it all. And he would have done that had he been in class with his students, but here in the market he decided it was more poignant than pointed, and he bought his food and left.

"Are you hungry, kids?"

"Starved."

"Not really."

"Well, help yourself, as you wish."

Jason dove into one of the bags and pulled out a sack of Doritos, which he ripped open with his teeth.

"I love these," he announced to no one in particular.

"There are some ham-and-cheese sandwiches in the other bag."

Jason found them and tossed one each to his father and to Rebecca.

"I said I wasn't hungry, vacant brain."

"Aw, man, she gives me indigestion. I'm gonna go check out the lake."

He left a trail of Doritos in his hasty path, and his shoes kicked dust onto the sheet. Rebecca jumped and brushed them all away with a sardonic "Jesus Christ" and a sigh of exasperation.

"He's only a child," David reminded her.

"Since when are you so sensitive to children's needs?"

"Must we start at zero today again, Rebecca?"

But she hadn't heard him. Her eyes were fixed on a woman near a bench by a cluster of trees. At first it appeared that she was doing some sort of little dance, or else practicing t'ai chi. But on second glance it was clear that her private pantomime was intended for eyes and voices that she alone could perceive.

They stared like shameless voyeurs.

She was a gaunt lady, close to David's age, with a thatch of strawberry curls uncombed and darting out from her scalp. Her hands were folded in pliant supplication, as if she were praying or begging for mercy. She mouthed a passionate oration without sound or speaker. As if on cue she jolted to her feet and pressed her palms together and rolled her eyes heavenward, pitching her violent oration to the angry, silent gods overhead.

Then, just as rapidly, she let her hands fly open and flap by her side like limp butterfly wings desperately fanning the stillness of the air. When her flutter was exhausted, she spun herself around, three complete rotations—both of them counted to themselves—then ran like a starved heron to seek solitude on the bench.

It was a matter of minutes before the sequel was repeated. The woman did not appear to be fatigued. No traces of perspiration or heavy breathing were apparent. Each performance was as zealously delivered as the one previous. David wondered how long she had been there.

Was this open-air theater her daily forum of despair?

"That woman is disgusting!" Rebecca grunted, seizing her sandwich but not removing her eyes from the spectacle.

"No, Rebecca, you are wrong. That woman is not disgusting; that woman is sad. Can you in any way recognize that there is a fundamental difference between the two?"

He wounded her with his words and his disapproving tone. He could watch with detached lucidity as she entered her sulk. It failed to move him.

"That disgusting woman, as you so cavalierly label her, is probably acting out a drama of pain that you or I would be incapable of bearing. Perhaps her children are dead, her spouse is in jail, her mother despised her, her father defiled her; maybe it's cancer or polio or blindness or retardation. Possibly a loved one went mad with jealousy and murdered or maimed, or it could be that a fire smothered or a flood drowned someone close to her, or maybe a car crash crippled her loved ones or snuffed them out, or perhaps the weight of history crushed her— or maybe, just maybe, life is too goddamn tragic for her to stand. Whatever the cause, it's most undeserving of the contempt of a sixteen-year-old snippet whose brains and bitchiness prevent her from having the slightest feeling for anyone else."

Tears rolled down her face, which was twisted in hurt and confusion. For a moment he felt a twinge of regret; he had not intended such a vitriolic outpouring, but it had simply avalanched out of him.

"You read the books, Rebecca. Surely you understand

when Dimmesdale mounts the scaffold to show his broken heart to the darkness. And I'm positive you didn't laugh at Miss Havisham, sitting there like a fool in her wedding dress.

"There's a connection, you know. Those stories mean something, after all."

She cried into her ham sandwich, silently, sobbing out her shame.

The woman continued her melancholy melodrama to the sporadic stares of passersby and the occasional mockery of children at play.

David stared off at the manmade lake, half-heartedly settling his eyes on the blond head of his son among the crowd of eager, sweltering youngsters.

"David?" Rebecca solicited cautiously.

"Hmm?"

"I don't have any friends."

15

I'd like to know just who he thinks he is, Mr. Returning Father, with his dramatic entrance like Jack Nicholson in *Batman*. Both of them make me sick the way they hog the spotlight, then pretend they don't know what's going on. Honestly, what do these guys take us for, anyway, airheads who can't see what's only obvious? When he came to get us the other day, Mom was cold to him. What a burn! He deserved it, waltzing in there like he owned the place or something. She just ignored him, which I loved, because he got nervous and started asking a lot of stupid questions like "What's that?" or "Where's Roger?"—as if he cared. He didn't think I saw all that but I did, and the best part was Mom making him squirm by saying nothing. She looked so pretty sitting there on the rug doing her work. She dressed up for him, I know, because she never wears eyeliner on the weekends, and she had some on. Still, the way she ignored him was wonderful because it made Mr. Controlovich nervous, and it's about time. He's always so sure he's right about everything. I think it's because he's a teacher and he reads a lot of books and talks well, so nobody questions him. Mr. Sneed doesn't do that to us, and he's real intelligent and reads books. Maybe he doesn't do that because we don't ignore him, at least not in the same way that Mom did. It's easy not to pay attention in class and look like you are.

Mom just didn't give him a chance. Maybe it's her way of getting back at him. She's always telling me to just ignore Jason and he'll bug off. But with Jason it's not the same, because he's so stupid he wouldn't know the difference. I'm basically a nonviolent person except with him, because words don't work, he doesn't understand them. If I ignored him, he'd probably be happy or not even notice.

Boy, David noticed. Kids at school do that sometimes. They call it the silent treatment, where nobody talks to you at lunch or break. They've done it to me. I don't care, they're all a pack of pigs, except for Julie Cohen. The one time she did it with the other kids, I really felt bad. Mom got that one out of me like she always does by nosing around until I tell her what's wrong. Some things are none of her business, but I know she doesn't like to see me hurt, which is a pretty nice thing about her. She doesn't think I know why she does it, but I do. I know it bothers her that Roger favors Jason, and she tries to make it up to me. I wish I could tell her that they *all* favored Jason, and she can't do anything about it. Everyone plays favorites, it's no secret. Roger likes me okay, but not like he loves Jason, because we're so different. I wish I could tell Mom that I've known that since the beginning and it's nothing new. What she wouldn't understand at all or she'd take the wrong way is that I don't want Roger that close to me, because it would be too phony. I'm not like him and I don't even pretend to be. I like him okay, but I don't want to be a surfer girl or watch TV like those cozy little families in the movies. I guess the real truth is that we tolerate each other because we both love Mom. It gets confusing sometimes, but I know that Mr. Sneed really likes me because he sort of knows what I'm like on the inside. Roger doesn't have a clue, and that's fine with me, because I get the impression that I'd wind up explaining all the time and he'd never understand anyway.

Mr. Sneed one time was discussing *The Effects of Gamma Rays on Man-in-the-Moon Marigolds* (which I loved) about having expectations that will never come true because the people you want things from aren't capable of giving them. Like Tillie and her mother, Beatrice, who's always saying she hates the world and Tillie has to listen, even though she doesn't believe it. Tillie found science and a teacher who showed her other ways of looking at things like atoms and stuff. I don't mean to say that Roger's a drunk or a loser or anything like that. He's not. He just goes about his life like Jason does; they just do things without asking too many questions. I'm sure not like that. My head is always full of questions. Sometimes I wish it weren't so filled up with thoughts, but that's just me. Mr. Sneed knows that. So does Mom. That's why she butts into my room and pokes around, because she knows when something's up. I can tell her things, but certainly not everything. When I'm mad I'm always tempted to ask her why she married Roger, but I don't dare because it would hurt her feelings, and I don't want to do that to her. It's funny, but I know exactly why she married David, although he certainly turned out to be a shithead. I can see them as a young couple, and I'll bet they were madly in love and they chopped each other down just to provoke emotion. David's handsome, but not all that great, but it's his style that's attractive, the way he says stuff with irony and humor sort of like Mr. Sneed, only better. He sort of reminds me of that old guy from the movies and commercials who put everybody down, but in a way that was mean but elegant. Mom told me his name is Sir John Gilgood and that he was a theater guy from way back. David sort of reminds me of him, only younger. I know that's supposed to be "charisma," but that word applies to many people, if you ask me. David's mind is sexy even though his mouth is mean. I know my mom is a lot smarter than she acts with Roger, and that makes me mad sometimes. I think she doesn't talk about a lot of stuff because Roger will feel left out or something. I bet she and David talked about *everything* and that she never felt he'd be left out. But then he left. It must have been because of me and Jason and all the boring stuff like baby cribs and creams, but still, what a shitty thing to do. And now she lets the son of a bitch come back to what he ditched in the first place! I just don't understand him at all. I don't think he cares one hoot about us. I think he came back to see *her*. Now that we're older, he probably figures she'll fall all over him again. Ha! She ignored him and was even rude. Tough for him; who cares? I certainly don't, and Jason is too dumb to see anything but what's in front of him on TV. David pisses me off with his "I'm trying to begin something here" routine. What a joke. It's like that thing that one of Jason's retarded buddies is always saying: "You grew it, you chew it." He made his bed, as they say, so why didn't Mom just let him lie in it? I think she still has a thing for him and that's why she gets all cold and mad. I know that sometimes when I feel funny about somebody, I get mean even if I don't want to. It keeps them away so they can't get close. Maybe Mom doesn't want to let David close because it's too dangerous. All this love stuff makes me tired. Roger and Jason are the types who seem to just sail on through with friends and family, and it's all just so easy.

I don't think love is easy. I mean, look what happened to Cordelia with her father because she told the truth, not like her phony sisters who faked it. I know that I'm not easy to love. Neither is David. But one thing bothers me, and I keep thinking about it. I'd never tell *anyone* this, not even Mr. Sneed, although I bet he'd agree. Maybe someday I'll tell Julie Cohen, but not now. It's something I think about, especially when I read books about complicated people like Holden Caulfield or Kate in *The Taming of the Shrew*. I never thought she was a bitch, and I don't care what the rest of those kids thought.

I think people who are hard to love are more worth the effort than the easy ones. I'm sure everybody would jump all over me about that and tell me I was being a snot or defending sarcastic people, but I really feel that.

It's like Roger or Jason. In a way they are easy to love because they don't pose any problems cuz it's all there in front of you. Like Disneyland, nothing to figure out. Personally, if that's what love is, you can have it. It's just too boring for me. I like to discover things about people and be surprised, because you have to hunt for buried treasure. It's like what happened at school with Julie Cohen the day I told the class that I thought Franny in *Franny and Zooey* was wonderful, and not a sulky pain in the ass like they all thought she was. Boy, everyone jumped on me about "what right did she have to come crashing home, take over the living room couch and announce to the world that she was having a nervous breakdown?" All I said was she had *every* right, because she finally found out that life was awful and shitty and she wanted off the train. Just because the rest of the world didn't understand, that wasn't her fault. Everybody booed me and said I was a cynic and spoiled and all this other stuff. I tried to explain how wonderful I thought it was that Zooey called her on the phone to talk to her about the little old lady in red sneakers with cancer, but they didn't hear a word I said. So I got mad and shut up. At break, Julie Cohen came up to me and said, "Know what I think?" and I said, "Who cares?" and she said "You do, and I think the world needs more people like you." God, I loved her at that minute. I wish I could have said something, but I didn't know what to say except cry and ask her to please be my friend. But I just couldn't get it out. That's what I mean about my being hard to love.

Am I worth the trouble?

Nobody's ever really taken the time to find out, so I guess I'll just have to wait.

David's certainly not on any expedition. God, he makes me sick, yelling at me in the park as if he were my real father and had the right to lecture me about things like compassion and empathy. What does he know about anything? He dumped us like yesterday's luggage, and then he snakes his way on back to crawl into our hearts, which are supposed to melt like chocolate fondue. I've got news for him.

Maybe Jason's all lovey-dovey and ready to let him invade like a Valentine card, but not me. Jason's stupid. I'm not. Mr. Morality Mouth bailed out on us, and I for one refuse to forgive and forget like he was Father Knows Best or something. Well, he's not.

I think he's probably hard to love too. But I don't know if he's worth it. Some things about him I sort of like. He notices things like beauty and meaning, and when he's not playing weekend warlock I sort of like listening to him talk. I look like him, which kind of makes me mad because his sort of looks go better on a man than a woman. His low eyebrows make him look intelligent. Mine look like a gash of wild hair growing straight across my forehead like a scar. His eyes are the same color as mine, and we have similar hands. Jason got all the prettiness from Mom. Nothing makes sense.

This whole scene makes me sick. Last spring at school Julie Cohen brought a family photo album of the big Passover seder they had for all the relatives. There were scads of relations all seated together at the table with the candles and all. Her parents are older. They've been married for thirty-five years and according to her are "still in love," whatever that means. All her brothers and sisters are older and married. Some of them even have children, which means Julie's already Aunt Julie at sixteen. How weird!

Anyway, after that awful Sunday in the park with that miserable man, I went home and went straight to my room to avoid the twenty questions I knew Mom would ask, like she always does. Sure enough, she came barging in.

"Have a good time, honey?"

"Not especially."

"What happened?"

"Nothing."

"Why are you upset?"

"I hate the guy, and you make me see him."

"Rebecca, he's your father."

"Some father."

"Isn't he trying to be nice?"

"He doesn't know how."

"Did you argue?"

"He did."

"And that made you sad?"

"It pissed me off, if you want to know the truth. Just like you were when he came to get us today."

"I wasn't angry."

"Liar. You were rude, and I loved it. But you make *us* be nice."

"Why don't you give him a chance?"

"He had his chance years ago, and here we are."

She got quiet after that and just kissed me good night and said she was sorry that he'd made me sad. I didn't say anything, and then she stood up and said something real softly. "He made me very sad too, Rebecca. But it passes, if you give it a chance."

I cried when she left, not because of what she said or that it had been such a terrible day—well, maybe a little of that, but that's not the main reason.

I just lay there in the dark thinking about all this whole thing, and Julie Cohen's Passover album kept coming into my head. I don't even know why. We're not Jewish or anything, but a lot of kids at school are. I just kept remembering this one picture that Julie held up to show us of the immediate family, as she called it. Her mom and dad were in the center holding hands, and all the kids formed a sort of semicircle around them, like a crescent. Her two older brothers stood behind their parents, all tall and proud and handsome. Julie and her sister Rachel flanked the sides. They were all smiling and happy like one of those Reach Out and Touch Someone ads.

"This is us all together," Julie said proudly. "Thirty-five years' worth."

I just kept thinking about that photo, and it made me cry even more. All my feelings got all stirred up. I hated everything, especially David Bartholomew and his yelling at me, and Roger's niceness and Jason's stupidity and Mom's weird motivation to put us all through this. Then I calmed down and it all fell into place like it always does if I think hard enough.

It was Julie's family picture, after all.

It should have been us.

16

When Abbie Hoffman had died and the coroner ruled it suicide from an overdose, David had despaired. Today, for some reason, he thought about it obsessively all morning.

Hoffman had been only three years his senior—wilder, more charming, more successful, and, David thought, happier. Certainly his outrageous, colorful antics had helped spice up a crucial decade.

David had always identified with him in his secret boudoir of vanity. He liked to think of himself as having the same tough but tender visage whose lines were wise and well earned. He fancied his voice gravel-toned and rich with fluid deepness. When he would lecture in class, sometimes he would pretend he was the worn and weary radical, out there slogging it out in a hostile world that lacked justice and beauty, but his tenacious toughness would allow him to endure.

He often fantasized that if someone made a movie of his life, Abbie Hoffman would play him.

There was a kinship there, David thought; it was the degree to which, despite the crowds, he could relate to the role of the ultimate loner.

David loved the idea of the tragic loner, the victim of unjust ridicule in a society that did not understand him.

Like Kafka's heroes, David featured himself as a man dragged out of bed and accused of things he had not done. And like all of Kafka's victims, his tormentors were also unknown, unidentified for specifics and details. He only knew that, like Hoffman, he also ran, often on a treadmill, from hostile forces that threatened his happiness. Why had he killed himself? It had signaled the end of an era.

Like Hoffman, he was the existential wanderer—brooding, contemplating, languishing the nuances of a complicated and unenlightened world that placed all the wrong emphasis on all the wrong values. He'd never missed the chance to watch his soul mate on the screen and forget the realities of a pouting husband and hesitant father. Hoffman had understood these things.

He was sure of that.

He sat in Hamburger Hamlet and thought about him. He wasn't sure of anything anymore. Part of him wondered if he wasn't pathetic. He certainly felt older around Jason and Rebecca.

"Hi, sugar buns! Fancy catching you in a hangout for hungry salesmen!"

His silent vigil was interrupted by the twangy cacophony of Doris Jean's shriek. She looked different in the daylight—older, but softer, more rounded and full. He smiled a tender recognition.

"What in hell happened to you?"

"Just thinking about Abbie Hoffman."

"Oh, him. I remember. He was too young to just crump like that. Did you know him in real life?"

He wanted to beg her to define real life for him, to give clear and concise examples—concrete, solid, sure, there.

"Let us just say that I was an ardent and faithful admirer."

"Boy, me too."

"It was his style that got him so far."

"He was one hell-raiser, that's for sure," said Doris Jean.

"Yes, but he believed," mused David.

"In what?"

"Better ways to live."

"His personal life was a mess."

"Aren't they all?"

"No. Some folks got it down."

"To what?"

"Boredom, I guess. Hell, don't ask me."

"Me either," David said, mournfully.

"You got that right, sugar."

"No, I don't."

"Well you're tryin'. That counts for something."

"Precisely what has yet to be determined. This is not Soon to Be a Major Motion Picture."

"Life ain't a movie."

"Indeed."

"Still, he shouldn't have checked out."

"Perhaps; he was brave."

"Bullshit; it's better to stick around and see what happens."

"Maybe."

"Say, what's goin' on with you?"

"Do you really want to listen?"

"Buy me some coffee, sugar. I'm all ears."

He told her about Jason's furtive visit and the evening they had spent together. It occurred to him in the retelling that his description of his son's lack of social grace was less harsh, even colored to appear affectionately caustic. With surprising compassion he recounted Jason's plaintive request that he not screw up his family—well, at least his voice was devoid of rancor.

"What about your daughter? She sounds like the pistol."

"Her utter loathing for me has somewhat calcified into a sort of galvanized contempt."

"Talk English, for Christ's sake."

"She hates me less, I think."

"What makes you think that?"

"She opened up to me about her life. Guardedly, of course, but I was able to fill in some of the blanks."

"Like what?"

"Like she has no friends to speak of. She hates and envies her brother, who apparently has a wonderful social life."

"Why doesn't she have friends? That ain't normal for a girl her age. Hell, I had a bucket of buddies in high school. We rode around and drank Cokes and raised hell. Never did a damn thing."

"Rebecca goes to a school for gifted children."

"That's your first mistake, right there."

"Why? She's a terribly bright young lady."

"Then she'd be bright anywhere. Why should you stick her with a buncha snots?"

"I'm not sure that's what it is. She reads wonderful books; I'm quite impressed, actually, with what she's read."

"So what? Ain't everything, you know."

"I know, but it's something, too."

"Hell, Sim Jabe gives a lotta money to some of those special schools. He does it as a tax write-off, but he sends me off to visit the place and he gets his picture in the paper as a great big deal."

"And?"

"I seen some of those kids, and I'll tell you, the brainy ones is the most pitiful."

"Why? Surely bright children are not excluded from the realm of personal happiness because of their gifts?"

"You talk like a goddamn book with a big title. That's not what I meant at all."

"Then what's your point?" he barked, but, softening, added, "I honestly don't understand."

"I know you don't, fruit fly; listen. Being brainy's fine, even real fine, if you get down to it; but being stuck together with people who think that's all there is stinks."

"I see. You object to the homogeneous grouping."

"Hot Christ and sheet. I do not object to homogenized whatever. What I'm sayin', buffalo breath, is that she ought to be able to just be a fool sometimes."

That he understood.

"You mean to lose herself to the rhythm of the moment."

"I mean so she can just ass around and have a good time."

He chuckled despite himself. His bladder ached from the pressure of six cups of coffee.

"I suspect my daughter has had previous little experience in assing around."

"Bingo, Ringo. She's probably afraid her teachers won't quiz her on it."

"Could be, could be. Mind you, she's not the most sympathetic child you'll ever want to meet. Sometimes I think she's cruel."

"Not enough assin' around. It all fits, angel baby."

"How can you be so sure, Doris Jean?"

"Believe me, sweetness, I ass around—speaking of which, what are you doin' for the next couple of hours?"

"I expect I'll accompany you to my motel."

"I was hopin' you'd say that. Let's go one round for Mr. Hoffman."

She had tried all day, but erasing David from her fantasies had been impossible. She had dreamed about him last night, an erotic, disturbing scenario that had left her feeling vaguely guilty and somewhat aroused. She remembered details long ago smothered in rage and bitterness. It alarmed her that she was able to recall the smell of his skin crushed against hers, the feel of the stubble of his chin wedged in the slope of her neck. She recollected the sighs and the murmurs with unnerving accuracy.

Slowly and cautiously she phoned Roger, explaining a little too eagerly that a producer had arrived from Canada and she would be having dinner in town. He had not doubted her sincerity.

She opened the bottom drawer of her desk to get her purse. It occurred to her that perhaps she should call first, but no.

In his arrogance, he would be expecting her. She

reached for the phone and quickly dialed the familiar number.

"Rebecca, hi honey, it's me. I have a business meeting tonight. Be sure and fix something for the boys."

"Why do I have to do it?"

"Because I need your help, sweetie."

"Right."

He told Doris Jean about the picnic in the park, their stroll through the impressionists at the museum, and the visit to the tar pits.

Rebecca had recognized most of the works of Degas and Cézanne. She had spoken with knowledge about Monet and Pissarro.

Jason couldn't wait to get out of there.

"Too boring, man. I mean, everything's dead in there."

In a sense, David supposed, he was correct.

"Roger much prefers my brother," she had confided to him. "They do everything together, most of it stupid and mindless, if you want to know the truth."

He felt the ache of her words, the spleen of the outsider.

The children fought all the way home. Sam did not invite him in. She had greeted her children and closed the door without so much as a wave.

"You got any hooch at your hotel?"

"That can be arranged."

"Good. I feel like a couple good belts before I loosen yours."

Her words stirred him. He could feel the swelling in his loins.

They embraced before the door was closed completely. His tongue probed the inside of her mouth, which tasted of coffee and breath mints.

"Call for ice, precious. I got private business in the bathroom."

He telephoned the cretin who had given him so much trouble about his messages. David's request was recorded with a promise of Right away, sir.

David took off his shoes and his jacket. He fingered the bottle of Johnny Walker, making note of the red label she'd chosen over the black.

"Ta da!" Doris Jean sang into the lath-and-plaster walls. She had stripped down to what looked like a lacy corset, the kind Dietrich wore in *Blue Angel*, garments that drove Emil Jannings to distraction and ruin.

"Like it? I bought it at the Tushery in Hermosa Beach."

"I think it's scintillating."

"It's called a teddy. I bought it in honor of the Kennedys and to wear whorin' around."

"You are smashing, Doris Jean. The desk clerk will agree with me, I'm sure."

He answered the timid knock, pulling a crisp dollar bill from his pocket. Doris Jean struck a pose she'd memorized from the fan magazines.

Sam stood there alone.

It took her a full thirty seconds before she'd absorbed every detail of the scenario before her.

"Oh, sweet Christ, Samantha. This is not what it looks like."

She turned on her heel and walked away.

"Absolutely nothing's changed," she hissed to the pavement underfoot.

17

He ran after her in his stocking feet.

"Sam, please, come back. I can explain."

"You miserable son of a bitch!" she yelled into the U-shaped courtyard. "Don't even open your callous, lying, fucking, stupid, shallow mouth."

He bolted and caught up with her. She freed her arm from his plaintive grasp.

"Get your fucking hands off me," she ordered coldly.

"Please, Sam, we need to talk."

"I've nothing to say to you, you bastard. Besides, you're busy."

"I can explain—honestly."

"You have nothing to explain about your cheap habitual activities. I came here to have you explain other things."

Her regard sizzled with hatred. He'd not recalled a volcanic aggression in her.

It seemed odd to experience Samantha's fury in the absence of wails of children, the constant accompaniment of their fights in the past.

She shivered with rage toward this man she could not possibly have loved.

"Please stay, Samantha. Just give me a minute. I want to talk to you about the kids."

"Everything you do and say smacks of selfishness and ends with someone getting hurt!"

"You don't mean that."

"You cannot possibly imagine how much I mean that, David."

Doris Jean had scuttled into the bathroom to dress, which she did, hurriedly. This was not the first time she'd been caught by an angry spouse or relative.

She assumed Samantha was the children's mother. Years of experience had taught her to read rage in such a way as to pinpoint the source.

He was a nice enough fellow, she reasoned, but he was a loser of a husband and a friend. Most of them were, in her opinion. The more she pleasured herself with others, the more she decided old Sim Jabe was okay—for a man, anyway, which wasn't saying much, since long ago she'd figured them to be mostly worthless creeps.

Sometimes she wondered why she bothered sleeping with them.

"Assin' around," she concluded, "the assin' around keeps me young."

They were hurling insults at each other in the parking lot now. The woman held her arms at her side with her fists clenched.

She could see him slump into a heap of despair. He

is awfully stupid, for such a bright fellow, she thought, and weighed the possibilities of rescuing him, or at least trying to.

She knew from the first night they met that he still loved his wife and kids. And that was the trouble, she'd thought; they love 'em but don't know what the shit to do about it from there.

She felt sorry for David. He was a man who wore his loneliness like a beat-up badge.

She decided to risk it, and slipped out the door and into the parking lot.

They were still yelling at each other.

"Listen!" she shrieked in her highest, most voluminous voice. Both of them turned to stare at her, but she relegated her piercing eyes to Samantha's face.

"Listen, sugar, you gotta believe this: I don't mean one thing to him."

"None of them ever do," Samantha answered coldly. "I didn't either."

Doris Jean could not think of a rejoinder, so she stole away quietly and looked for the nearest bus stop.

"You didn't have to be rude, Sam."

"I'm not obligated to be polite to your whores, David. Not any more."

"That woman is not a whore, Sam."

"*All* women are whores in your eyes, David."

"There's no need to become a martyred moralist."

"Fuck you and your morals and your lies. Don't you ever get sick of using people?"

"I don't use people. Passion is a two-way street, if you haven't totally forgotten."

"I know all about your shallow, hollow passion, David. I haven't forgotten a thing."

"What is that supposed to mean?"

"It means that time makes you forget the sting, but I remember every rotten, lousy, stinking, selfish move you ever made."

"Is that what you came to tell me?"

"There's nothing I could tell you that you haven't already done. Strangers, colleagues, close friends—it's all the same to you."

Both of them knew what she meant.

Shirley Kunzel. Doctor Shirley Kunzel, professor of contemporary lit at B.U., concerned faculty adviser, committee woman, and David's lover.

It had taken Sam months to put that one together. She'd genuinely liked the woman, who was a damn sight more humane than the rest of his colleagues, dreary drones with their bored, depressed wives sitting primly around their apartment when it was their turn to entertain. She'd dreaded those evenings—heavy, tense, monotonously predictable ordeals. The men would pontificate, offer some tedious sermonette whose implied message was My theory tops yours, while their hostile, morose wives sat quietly listening to the orations they'd heard so often.

Shirley was different; she would lighten up the evening with laughter, occasionally poking fun at the sacrosanct pomposity of one of the more fatuous professors.

She asked about the kids and listened with genuine interest. Without being asked, she would rise and help clean up, making acrid comments to the lazy, assuming males who, sprawled in their chairs, continued to eat and smoke.

San had honestly liked her.

She didn't know exactly when she'd figured it out. It was nothing either one of them ever said or did. It was a look she'd interrupted—intercepted, actually, like a phone message or a billet-doux given to the wrong person.

They were at their apartment. Another dreary departmental get-together in celebration of someone's tenure.

Peter Kaminsky, the medieval scholar, was expounding on one of his pet theories about the Middle Ages. He argued that courtly love as known in the twelfth and thirteenth centuries was essentially more free and joyous than the liaisons of the liberated libidos of the swinging '60s.

"It's quite uncomplicated, actually. Marriage was nothing more than a social arrangement based on lineage and private property."

Heads nodded like bobbing apples at a carnival, as the small audience tried to confirm that they too had a historical backdrop for literature.

"So, then, love was essentially adulterous, playful, unattached, allowing an uncomplicated arena sans hearth and home, where pure, plentiful lust could take place."

He smiled smugly and continued.

"One need only look at the faces in the paintings, hear the words of the *chansons de geste.* It's all recorded for eternity. These happily amoral lovers could scarcely contain their joy."

It was then she had caught it, the slight alarm in Shirley's eyes, the awesome recognition of their private joy so clearly registered in his, the charged exchange of those who share an intense and dark secret.

She guessed it then, and it had broken her heart.

"I want you to know, Samantha, that I do not do those things any more."

"What you do, David, is of little concern to me."

"I suppose you're correct there," he conceded.

"What does affect me, however, is what's happening with my children."

"Our children; you said 'my children.' "

"I know what I said. It's hard to think of them as ours."

"I must admit, Sam, that I share your disquietude."

"What do you mean?"

"I've been here long enough to register Jason's utter disinterest in studies, and to say that Rebecca is a hostile, ill-behaved adolescent is an understatement."

It took her a moment to react to the impact of his words, and when she could rescue her scattered thoughts, she was yelling at him.

"You arrogant motherfucker! Don't you *dare* insult those children! How *dare* you even begin to pass judgment on them!"

"Sam, what I said is quite apparent to the most superficial observer."

"What do you know about anything? You dumped out on those kids, leaving them high and dry, and you come back here to give grades on their progress in life? Go fuck yourself, David Bartholomew! You're lucky they even talk to you!"

"From what I hear from Miss Congeniality, they've been forced to."

"Not anymore. You've done enough. Rebecca screams at me when I remind her she's to see you!"

"Why are you screaming this at me now, here, in the middle of a parking lot?"

Indeed, they were quite a spectacle, carrying on like noisy fishmongers. People listened from inside the motel rooms. Two maids stationed themselves in the laundry

room, from where they had followed this urban melodrama from the beginning. People on the street who had
caught fragments of "motherfucker" and "fuck yourself"
stood aimlessly around, waiting for the next installment.
David tried lowering his voice, which only served to
make Samantha augment hers. She yelled at the top of
her lungs.

"Why should *you* always be the person who makes
up the rules? I'll yell wherever the hell I goddamn well
please!"

"Yeah!" the maids agreed in unison.

"Can we go inside and talk, Samantha?"

"Sure, David, but I'm afraid I left my slut's garb at
home!"

"Samantha, we need to talk about our children."

"I know," she spoke in a normal tone of voice. The
onlookers strained to hear the hushes. "We need to talk
about lots of things, David."

"I know. Please come inside. I promise to remain
civilized."

"I don't," and she laughed a little, mostly from
tension, but a little at herself, too.

He fidgeted with the knob while she waited silently
by his side, aware that entering a motel room with one's
former spouse was not without its wicked irony.

He put his hand across the doorway to block her
entrance.

"I want one thing to be clear, Samantha. What you
said was a lie. You never 'meant nothing' to me."

"Stop it, David."

He looked pathetic for an instant, small and old. He
took a deep breath and kept his arm firmly planted on
the doorjamb.

"There was a time, Samantha, when you meant the world to me." He released his grip.

"That was then, David. This is now."

He shut the door and locked it, out of habit.

 **18** "Would you care for a drink?"

"No, thank you."

She scanned the room for the current objects of his life. She could find nothing remotely familiar, no nagging accoutrement of memory. The strangeness relaxed her.

There was no link to her past in this room save the man who was once both its nucleus and its zenith.

She sat at the fake wood table, as far away from the bright floral-spreaded bed as she could manage. The heat of the afternoon caused her legs to stick to the vinyl of the chair.

"Why did you come here, David?"

"I assumed I'd sufficiently explained why."

"Don't assume a thing, David. Why did you come?"

"Because I'm a lonely man who would like to know his children."

"Why now? They were your children five years ago, ten years ago, last month."

"There's no need for sarcasm, Samantha. You asked me a simple question and I told you the truth."

She'd always mistrusted David's truths, and now was no exception. The core of dishonesty she had so feared and blocked from her souvenirs burned its way into her mind like smoldering acid. He must have suspected something; his eyes betrayed him. He stared at her tresses, which reminded him of sensuous seaweed in calm waters. He would have liked to reach across and touch her; the draining melancholy of the moment warned him to beware.

"I have always despised your truths, David. Somehow your verities turn into stab wounds."

"Are you happy, Samantha?"

"It's none of your business, David. Yes, I am happy."

"Fair enough."

"No, it wasn't fair at all, David. What I have now was earned right out of a pit of unfairness."

"You have the children."

"I have always had the children, David, right from the beginning."

Her voice was shrill, controlled, accusatory.

"I never lied to you about them, Sam."

"You never wanted them at all!"

"That's true. I never denied it."

"And you never failed to show us, either, did you?" A bubble of hot poison rose in her throat.

"Ah," he sighed impatiently, "the chimes of guilt, a carillon of culpability. Did you ever contemplate my side?"

"For years, David, I tried to unravel it. My conclusion was that you didn't have one, except that your steady

muse was no longer available when some winsome coed
grew tired of your charms, or when you felt it was time
for a new toy. You never valued any of us, David. You
don't know how to value people. No wonder you talk
your fancy passionate theories; you're incapable of being
anything but a superficial skimmer."

A bitterness oozed into her voice, choking her air.
She could smother here with him. He reached across the
table and put his hand on hers. A shiver of excitement
surged through her. She could see the veins of his temples
pulsating, throbbing with hurt. He lowered his voice to a
stage whisper.

"I loved you with a craziness that has never left me.
You smelled like trees, all woodsy and fresh, and you
tasted like ripe, sweet apricots. You could never understand my famished joy at having found you."

She ripped her hand away from his and bolted to her
feet, screaming, "That's bullshit, David! You and your
trees and fruits and airy murmurs. You said you loved
me, and you left me with a barrelful of romantic homilies
and two kids to raise on my own!"

"I never wanted it that way."

"Right; I know all about your wants. You wanted a
muse to paint bleak portraits and kiss your ass and listen
to stark theories on grand passion! You wanted an audience for your orations about feelings you didn't have,
sentiments you couldn't express, and love you were incapable of giving. You wanted a passioniate handmaiden
who'd be your mother and not cramp your style."

"And you wanted a house and a home and chintz
curtains and a station wagon."

"Fuck your patronizing platitudes about love. You
don't know the first thing about love!"

"And your muckle-mouthed insurance executive has elevated you to the pinnacle of passion?"

She slapped his face as hard as she could. He winced from the pain and smiled ever so slightly.

"That common man you so disdain was a lover who was there in the morning. You can't possibly imagine how much I despise you and all you represent."

"You think you have it all neatly worked out, don't you, Samantha? I was the heavy because I walked out the door. Did you ever for one second stop to wonder why I left? You inherited a foolproof role: martyred mother—better yet, abandoned martyred mother. Sighs of social sympathy as you clucked around lactating in a sea of self-pity. Did you ever consider that I despised what you represented?"

Her hardness of spirit assaulted him with its violence. He reached over to touch her cheek, and she came at him with a fury. She dug her hands into his hair and yanked and tugged with a force he did not believe she could possess.

"You condescending prick—selfish, stupid asshole. How I wish you would die!"

He fought to free himself.

"Don't you dare talk to me like that," she raged. "I am no longer one of your adoring students."

"Indeed."

"Knock it off, David. Why did you come?"

"I wanted to see my children."

"And what brought about that sudden idea?"

"Possibly age, loneliness."

"You should have thought about that years ago."

"I had other things on my mind."

"Right. What female would be your next conquest."

"Is this going to be a moral argument?"

"You don't have morals, David."

"Are you my judge?"

"Yes, I was your fucking wife, you bastard!"

"Until you insisted on becoming Roseanne Barr in a mumu."

"I loved you, David, and I wanted your children."

"And I worshiped you and wanted you all to myself."

"Just like your father?"

"Let's not get into parents checking out. Your mother offed herself—that's desertion."

"You fucking asshole, my mother was desperate."

"So was I."

"Why, David, why? There was enough of me to go around."

"Don't make me laugh, Sam. You had no time for anything except Rebecca the second she screamed her way into this world. She's still screaming."

"Didn't it ever cross your mind that you have something to do with that?"

"Don't pull that guilt shit, Sam. She was impossible, and so were you and your dripping tits always waiting for her hungry mouth."

"You're sick to be so jealous of a baby."

"I lost my friend, my lover, my muse to that tribe of earth mothers cooing about organic vegetables and disposable diapers."

"You selfish prick. You couldn't share."

"Share what? Midnight wails and another child?"

"There is nothing wrong with being a family."

"We were a family."

"No, David, we were a couple of desperadoes clinging to each other for dear life in the hallowed halls of academia."

"And you had to fuck it up."

"I never lied to you. I wanted children."

"And you saw to it that you got them."

"They were your children too."

"I didn't want that kind of a family."

"Well, I did."

"And look at the cost."

"I lost you and I was heartsick, betrayed, and alone."

"You know I loved only you."

"And all the other women you were fucking."

"Because you were unavailable."

"Because you couldn't love your own family."

"Well, you have your tidy little family now. Are you happy?"

"Yes, David, I am."

"Then why did you let me come?"

"So you could get to know your children."

"My children. Those children would never be my children."

"Don't you dare criticize my kids."

"Now they're yours?"

"Where the fuck were you, David, when those kids needed you?"

"Not mucking around in mediocrity."

"My life is not mediocre, David. I have a life, a husband, a career, and happiness."

"Is that your definition of happiness?"

"Fuck you. If you only knew how I hate you."

"Listen, you bitch, you imposed those children on me! We had no money, I was just beginning. We had come from such horrid pasts to each other, and you just had to fuck it up!"

"I didn't make those children alone, you son of a bitch! It's normal to want love to grow like that!"

He flung her across the room. She threw a lamp into his face and followed it with the Gideon Bible.

"Since when do you author what's normal, Sam?"

The telephone book was her next airborne weapon.

"I like to clutter up a man's life. You're a person who spends his time tidying up, getting rid of people."

"Goddamnit, Sam, I wanted to be *yours*. I loved it that we were together—you were the first and only person who loved me back, and I wanted to keep you just for me," he added softly.

"I'm sick of your Painful Past speech, David. We all have painful pasts. You couldn't ever give yours up and live with us in the present."

"I didn't want those kids, Sam, I wanted *you*. The second you were pregnant, that was the end of you. You stopped reading, you never picked up a brush, you shut me right out of your life."

"And since you couldn't imagine helping me, or playing a part in our lives, you set out to make it horrible. I *did* try to go to school, a fact you've neatly forgotten. I wanted it all, David—you, art, babies, everything. You wanted a fan club of wallowing groupies to hang on your every word."

"That's not true!" he protested bitterly.

There was a curative balm in her anger; the flashes of hostility invigorated her, tensed and relaxed her into opening the floodgates.

"You fucked every woman in our lives. Useless, angry humping! Did you think that I didn't know?"

He held a chair up to ward off flying objects sailing at him with force and regularity.

"You set half of those up! I couldn't even talk to you! Miserable little Rebecca would wedge her way between us, and you would become a nipple-dribbling earth mother!"

"I had to do something, asshole; you scarcely talked to her, and she adored you."

The veins in her neck stood out like topographical tributaries. Sobs choked out from her throat. He circled her like a distempered, prowling outlaw.

"I probably left no empty space when I left. Except for the fucking money, you most likely didn't even notice."

"Oh, you fucking vermin, if you knew how I hated you! Money! How *dare* you speak about money! There *wasn't* any, until your guilt or your lawyer forced you to have some decency. We did without, but we got by, no thanks to you. I found a job and spent half of my salary paying for child care for kids who could talk only about their father. Your daughter stood by the window and waited—for two years! Your son cried for you every night! While you were out finding your soul and fucking anything that flattered you, I was home with that."

"You martyred yourself, suffering motherhood. Botticelli's beauties rewarded in heaven for their selfless sacrificing! Good for you, Samantha. You got your reward."

"And so did you! Those children hate the very sight of you! Roger hates your guts, and I loathe everything about you!"

"Are you so sure about your little life?" Her words had wounded him terribly.

"My life is not little, David. I have a home, a family, and a career I adore. And I'm good at it."

"Let's hear it for your successes."

"No, let's hear it for your failures."

"Perhaps they're one and the same."

"Not a chance. Look at you, David. A pathetic middle-aged swain, groveling around after some cheap substitute for love. If you are here to play games with those children, let me warn you: It took me years to figure out that your games were the most interesting thing about you. I no longer find them interesting; they are deadly destructive, and tedious."

"And what are you, Sam, besides smug, sanctimonious, and self-satisfied? Is what you grovel after the real thing—a piece of the rock, so to speak?"

He reached for her head and she thrashed out to slap him again, but they fell exhausted into each other's fatigued embrace, and both of them sobbed, though for different reasons.

"Jesus Christ," he whispered into her hair, "what are we doing to each other?"

She could feel his arousal against her stomach. He put his arms around her back and she did not pull away. Slowly his hand caressed her torso into a flurry of I'm sorrys and other senseless murmurings. She choked back a sob and lunged her face into his like a hungry animal. His lips were soft and pliant as his tongue slithered its velvet smoothness into the familiar flesh of her mouth.

They tore at each other's clothes with a sensual sadness smothered by the melancholy of the moment.

His body did not seem strange to her. Her fingers refound the intimate landscape and retraced the worn topography of cries and whispers. David bent his head to find her breasts, familiar pleasure points; he breathed in her perfume. She reached for his cautiously and they began the crippled choreography of love that is over. The utter lack of joy caused Samantha to unleash passions as if they were weapons meant to destroy and maim. Beads of perspiration danced on his forehead as he pounded his fury into her and she rose up to meet him, clawing his back like a bird of prey whose talons pierce its victim as they soar through open space, final motions before the abrupt stillness of death.

They cried out like wounded animals and fell exhausted, tangled tarantulas in the threads of their own deception.

Neither of them made an attempt to move until it had turned dark outside, and Samantha stirred and freed herself.

She touched his face tenderly and kissed him gently on the cheek.

"Your children don't hate you, David. That was a lie meant to hurt you," she whispered into the damp sadness of the room. A cricket trilled its staccato aria somewhere in the corner. He said nothing for a while; then he turned to her and spoke without rancor.

"I am so confused, Sam. Absolutely nothing in my life has turned out as I would have it. I don't know what I'll do back in Boston, except wonder where I go from here."

She put her arms around him tenderly.

"I'm sorry, David. I really am. I want you to know that I did love you once; it's important that you know that."

He didn't get angry; he helped her wash her face and straighten her hair.

"I'm going home to my family now," she whispered without bristle or obvious self-satisfaction. Her voice was like an assemblage of specially arranged notes that would never be played again.

"Wait just a minute, Sam. I have something for you." He rummaged around to find his pants, took a piece of paper out and handed it to her.

"What's this?" she asked softly.

"Read it."

" 'Share, *Vb*. To enjoy or endure in common; participate in. To give a part of to another or others: usu. used
with *with*.' "

"That's why I came, Sam. I want to share with my
children."

The moon shined its merciless amber light on them.

"We'll see you Sunday, David. The children would
like that, since it's your last."

People fear the darkness, he thought to himself,
standing in the glow of evening. They are wrong; moonlight is the lucent revealer of lies and loneliness; it ignites
and kindles all of what we have suspected about ourselves.

19

Something weird is going on around here. One minute they're fighting and screaming about David the Dick, and the next minute they're grabbing around at each other, all lovey-dovey. It's thoroughly revolting. Roger looks like a dork when he's trying to be a stud. He gets this look on his face like he thinks he's Robert Redford or something, and he follows her around the house giving secret signals to her. He thinks we don't know what they mean. Adults really and truly make me sick.

I bet they've been doing it a lot lately. I've come to the conclusion that guys always want to do it when they feel jealous or insecure. How disgusting, when you think about it! Roger's been mooning around here like a lovesick cow. Poor Mom. I know she's been crying a lot lately. She doesn't know I know, but I do. I can tell when she's in the bathroom too long that she's been locked in there crying. Her eyes get all red and she says it's allergies, but she's lying and I know it. I bet it's his fault. Things have been weird since he got here. I wish I could talk to Mom about it. I'm afraid she'll get mad if I let on that I know. I'd like to tell her that I think I understand what's cooking around here.

He makes me cry, too. He has a way of making you feel shitty about things, like he's always right or something. The other day in the park I wanted to slap his face. Sometimes I think he has his nerve coming here like this. He says he's here to get to know us, but then where does he get off criticizing us? I can tell he thinks Jason's dumb. He doesn't say anything, but he's not happy about it. I guess in his job, he teaches kids who love school. Like me. Except most of the kids where I go to school gag me. They are boring, except for Mr. Sneed. He's nice, and besides, he's funny, even though half of the geeks in there never laugh at what he says. I do. He likes me. I can tell. Julie Cohen told me he's married to a lady scientist who writes books. They don't have any kids. I wonder if he makes her do it when he feels insecure. Maybe she tells him to leave her alone because she's busy with her theories. Still, I like him a lot.

The rest of my teachers make me sick. They walk around all serious and snotty. What they don't know is how boring they are.

I wish I had friends. Jason has tons of them, but I wouldn't get along with people like that. Julie Cohen's nice. She laughs at Mr. Sneed too. Maybe I should invite her to sleep over.

I think I've figured out what happened between them. Mom and David really loved each other. I bet they did it all. You can tell when you look at them, because they are afraid to look at each other. Each of them pumps me about the other. They think they're being so goddamn subtle. Quel joke! David asks all these indirect questions, like I'm not supposed to know what he's after. "What do you guys do at night, Rebecca?" Translation: "What does your mother do at night with that other guy?"

I wasn't born yesterday, after all. Sometimes I make up stuff to throw him off the track. "They disappear into their bedroom and all we hear are the yelps." He didn't seem amused.

Mom's not much better. "What's your father do all week between visits?" Translation: "Is he here with someone, and is it a woman?"

Adults are actually sort of stupid. Jason, of course, tells everybody everything. He just likes to talk.

Roger sure hates David. I can kind of understand why. It's like someone horning in and stealing your friend. Besides, David can be very shitty. I think I know why he makes Mom mad. He thinks he knows it all. He does know a lot, but he doesn't know everything.

I don't think he likes me. His tone is disapproving. Well, I've got news for him; I don't approve much of him either. I hate it when my mother cries, and somehow I'll just bet he's making her unhappy. Maybe his being here reminds her of before. It reminds me of that. Maybe he's sarcastic because he doesn't like how we've turn out.

Tough shit. I don't think I like him much. But I like Mr. Sneed. Essentially they're a lot alike. Except Sneed's not my father. In a sense, neither is this guy. I'll be glad when he goes home. Life's got to be easier than this.

They were lined up like lemmings, roped off with a red velvet cord marked ENTER on one end and EXIT on the other. The tellers at the window directed traffic as well as business. "Next, please," the nasal whine repeated in an orderly fashion to the impatient queue snaking its way around the lobby of the bank.

It must be payday, David surmised from the size of the crowd. This was normal fare for Boston, therefore it had to be unusual for California.

He tried waiting patiently; the lassitude of the tellers annoyed him on principle.

To ward off depression he'd stalked the bars of Westwood and picked up a diminutive coed named Wendy. She was a theater major who aspired to be the Bo Derek of family entertainment. She had a plan of action all worked out.

Instead of being a sex object, she contrived to promote a persona of *wholesome* sexuality, a natural kind of sensuousness the whole family could relate to.

He was fascinated by her game plan.

She would write a movie espousing love and marriage in which the wife who baked, cooked, scrubbed, and served was a drop-dead, knockout 10. Her husband and children loved her for this, and constantly photographed her and sent the snapshots in to contests, which she inevitably won. The victories sent swells of pride throughout the family, but she took the huge cash prizes and handed them over to charities like the arthritis telethon, where her pledge was read over the air to an audience of thousands.

Wendy wasn't sure what it all meant, but she knew that she would star in it and create everything from good feelings about sex to colorful beach towels with her picture airbrushed on the surface.

They'd gotten terribly drunk together and he'd taken her back to the hotel, where the entire staff was not unconvinced that this man from back east was running a brothel.

She had a jagged slash of a scar running diagonally across her torso.

"Gall bladder," she announced matter-of-factly. "The studio will have to pay to have that removed. I've already decided that will have to be written into the contract."

She was a brisk and efficient lover, as if each move was timed and planned for maximum efficiency and minimal effort.

He couldn't recall what she looked like.

"Next, please."

The woman with the glasses was addressing him. He approached her wearily, aware that he was hung over and tired. He pushed a money order onto the counter.

"ID," she commanded in a staccato burst.

He plunked his Massachusetts license down, which she scrutinized as if for prints.

"You're not a resident here?"

"Where? In this bank?"

"California, sir. Are you living in California?"

"I'm staying here."

He gave her the address of the motel. She eyed him suspiciously.

"This will take three days to clear. May we reach you at your motel during the day?"

"But it's a money order from my own account in Boston."

"Nonetheless, sir, it will take three days."

"But I'm a professor," he protested.

"We'd do the same for the President, sir. Rules are rules."

And he became unglued and made a scene.

He'd phoned Elizabeth several days before in despair and confusion over this debacle with Samantha. He needed money and sympathy. She tried to take care of both.

He related his story, and she listened with compassion and more than a few laughs. She reminded him that psychodrama was ultimately purgative and cleansing, and since he was in the land of acting out to just go with it and see what happened.

In the meantime, she promised to wire him three hundred dollars. She advised him to use part of the money to amass some research to show his judgmental colleagues that he had not pissed away a month baking in the sun.

He pressed her for details, and she provided them, and that depressed him even further.

She promised to meet his plane.

"This is absurd," he shrieked at the bank teller. "I want to see the manager immediately!"

"Whatever," she stated tersely, and went off to find a short, preppy-looking fellow with an inoffensive smile and a limp handshake.

The people in the line shuffled restlessly. Their sympathy with his plight did not offset their resentment at his holding up the line.

The manager scarcely managed to placate him. They haggled over policies and pettiness until someone from the crowd of curious spectators stepped forward to offer his assistance.

"What are you doing here, Roger?" David asked, sincerely shocked to see him.

"Estate settlement. Business. What's the hassle?"

"Do you know this man?" the manager inquired.

Alas, yes, both of them thought, and when Roger

wryly affirmed their connection, with no small glint of irony, they both laughed, a sort of nervous sniff.

He offered to act as a reference, and David got his money. He thanked Roger awkwardly as they wormed their way out of the bank.

"Forget it. It's my nature to be helpful. Besides, I can't get rid of you if you have no money."

He smiled and shrugged his shoulders in a half-hearted apology for such ungracious thoughts. David did not take offense; he laughed a bit nervously and offered his hand. He was sure Roger did not know about the fiasco with Sam.

Just as well, he thought to himself. It has nothing to do with him, actually.

They shook hands like civilized gentlemen, both of them a little proud of their maturity. All things considered, it did not feel so terrible being magnanimous.

"Say," Roger piped out, "have you had lunch yet?"

David shook his head to signal no, a strange malaise churning in his stomach.

"What say we go and have a pastrami on rye and a beer? There is a terrific deli around the corner."

David's puzzlement must have shown, because Roger sighed and picked up on it immediately.

"Look, it's only a sandwich, after all. You can pay, if it makes you feel more comfortable."

The California notion of comfort confused him. He could never imagine himself doing this, not given the circumstances.

"Say," he asked cautiously, "you're not going to threaten to rearrange my face again, are you?"

"Nope."

And he didn't.

Lunch was not altogether unpleasant, and instead of a black eye, David ended up with an invitation to a barbecue the next evening, which he accepted with just a glimmer of trepidation.

20

"Oh, Roger, you can't possibly be serious." Her voice nosedived into exasperation.

"Of course I'm serious. Trust me, Samantha; everything is fine, aboveboard."

"Did you go find him and work it out?" she asked, testing, pushing for details. She had offered no information about her own reunion. He'd asked about her sullen, swollen eyes, and she'd lied and told him that something had reminded her of her mother.

Jason watched this interaction with delighted confusion. Lately he'd begun to notice things he hadn't before. It had been almost automatic for him to side with his stepfather, who had been an unfaltering ally in the past. It was he who convinced his mother to let him try things she saw as dangerous, to relax about his absorption in the ocean, reassuring her that the verve to do that and little else would ease up a little. He was grateful to Roger, and fair is fair, so he would be inclined to favor his point of view about the others.

But lately he wasn't sure. Jason's careful observation over the past three weeks made him wonder if his mother didn't have a point.

Rebecca sloshed into the kitchen. Her hair was in tangles, and she had not bothered to put a robe over her Beethoven T-shirt. Jason groaned in agony as he cruised her white body and pantomimed vomiting. She pulled a hank of his hair with a vicious tug.

"Stop it!" Samanatha ordered, and turned back to Roger. "I think it's a perfectly terrible idea, and you should have consulted us."

"What's a terrible idea?" Rebecca demanded.

"He invited the other dude to the barbecue tonight," her brother answered.

"You're shitting me."

"Don't use that language in my kitchen!"

"Mom's pissed, too," Jason added, as an afterthought.

Rebecca checked to verify her mother's expression. Samantha scowled into the scrambled eggs, while Roger stood by in polite bewilderment.

"Why did you invite him, Mom?" Rebecca asked in a hostile tone.

"I didn't. Your father did."

"What the hell for?"

She peered at Roger, demanding an answer. He resisted the urge to slap her.

"Because I thought it would be a decent thing to do, all things considered."

"Did you fix him up with a date, too? Perhaps someone from your office; you guys could double."

"Don't get fresh, Rebecca. Your mouth always gets you into trouble."

Rebecca huffed to her seat and went into her sulk. Jason eyed her distastefully, and she yelled at him to cram it.

"Aw, man, how come everything gets so screwed up around here?"

"Because some of us don't use our brains."

"That's enough!" Roger snapped.

"This is weird," Jason spat out. His father softened and tried to explain himself more clearly.

"Look, he's leaving in a week. He came all this way to see you guys, and you've just visited with him on Sundays."

"That was the arrangement, Roger."

He did not acknowledge that remark and continued his rationale, which he only half-heartedly believed but felt compelled to defend.

"Listen, he's a stranger here and all alone. Why shouldn't we invite him to join us?"

"Oh, my god. You should like *The Sound of Music.* Where's Julie Andrews, I'm going to puke."

"Shut up, Rebecca."

"Look," Roger announced to the group, "what's the big deal?"

"It's no big," Jason concluded.

"The big deal," Samantha explained in clipped, articulated tones, "is that we don't want him, and you should have consulted us before extending your charitable good will."

"Charity! Listen, cookie; he's *your* ex-husband."

"Good point, Roger. Why do *you* feel guilty toward him?"

"Oh, for Christ's sake. If you ask me, you're all a bunch of stingy, selfish . . ."

"This entire thing is fucked!" Rebecca shrieked, running out of the room.

"Watch the eggs, Roger," Sam said, leaving to find her daughter. Roger looked at Jason, who was drinking in the confusion in great heaping gulps.

"Women," said Roger conspiratorially, "are a gigantic pain in the ass."

She was slouched in the corner of her bed, staring out the window. Sam knocked on the door, a habit she'd carefully cultivated with her children. Rebecca would not answer, so she tried again. When it was clear that she would not respond, she went in anyway.

"What happened to the rights of privacy?"

"It got erased by the rights of mothers."

"I'm not buyin' it."

"Me either."

She sat down on her daughter's bed with a soft thud. Rebecca squirmed and sighed, making it perfectly clear that her mother's presence was an enormous imposition.

"I'm not coming tonight, so don't try and beg me."

"Who's begging you?"

"You will be, I know you. In a few minutes you'll dump all this garbage on me about how he's my father and all that shit and that I owe him my presence. Well, forget it. I'm not coming."

"Me either. Shall we go to a movie?"

"Do you mean it, Mom?"

"Sure, why not? I didn't invite David to this. Your father did. Let him entertain him."

She smiled a wicked little grin that Rebecca did not fully comprehend. It was unlike her mother to be malicious, although she could not be sure that's what it meant.

"Why would Roger do that? He hates him."

"I think he feels sorry for him. He ran into him by accident and he was all alone and Roger felt bad for him."

"Do you hate him, Mom?"

"Which one?"

She laughed in spite of herself, and Rebecca smiled too.

"David Bartholomew."

"Do I hate him? No. Oh, I have my moments when I would like to see him pinned under a semi, but on the whole I'm beyond hate."

"What's that supposed to mean?"

She would have liked to tell her about the other day, to draw her into her circle of confidence where hidden hurts could be shared, and her daughter would become her friend. She sensed a soul mate in her, a woman like herself who would understand dark passions, deep slivers embedded in old wounds. She would have at least liked to tell her that they'd swung at each other, like the executioners of old, and severed the bloody roots of love once and for all. She would have liked to tell her the truth: that love doesn't die until you kill it off.

But this was her daughter, only sixteen, too young to know of such murderous doings. She put her arm around Rebecca and simply stated, "It means that it's over, sweetie. I have no strong feelings about him. He just is there."

Samantha silently reassessed her proclamation, which she decided approached close enough to the truth.

"Then why don't you want him to come?"

She thought about that for a moment. A good question.

"First of all, I didn't expect it. And second, it is a bit strange, although I'm sure it could be argued that it's not so odd. It doesn't feel right to me."

"Me either. Besides, he's a dick. I'm surprised Roger hasn't figure that out by now."

"I think he felt it for a bit, but now he just feels sorry for him."

"He should help the needy, not the greedy. David's always cutting me down."

"Your father's—David's—tone is often deceptive; he sounds worse than he is."

"Were you serious about ditching out on tonight?"

"I think so. Why, don't you want to now?"

"It would be a good burn; let the fellas all get together in a big, beer-drinkin' Budweiser brotherhood, and we'll boogie."

Rebecca smiled, her second of the day. Sam hugged her close.

"What do you supposed they'd talk about without us?"

"Jockstraps and sports scores and how many women they screwed."

"Rebecca," she teased, in a gentle reprimand.

"Well, it's true. They're so boring it's pathetic."

Someone rapped at the door. Neither got up to answer, but Samantha, in the interest of peace, voiced a pleasant "Yes?"

"I'm taking off now, Sam."

"As if anybody cares," Rebecca whispered to her mother, who signaled her to be quiet.

"I'm dumping Jason at the skateboard park. See you tonight."

"Okay." Sam spoke to the closed door.

"Aren't they weird, Mom—I mean, all of them?"

She lowered her eyes down to slits and spoke con-spiratorially.

"Men," said Samantha, "are a gigantic pain in the ass."

21

Everyone was oozing over with nervous smiles until the third round of margaritas had soothed them into a suspended state of tipsy relaxation.

"Aren't they disgusting?" Rebecca asked her brother, who sat next to her on the sand, quietly drinking in the strangeness of the evening.

The flicker from the camp fire Roger had expertly constructed danced odd configurations on their faces. Sam and David had avoided each other's gaze all night. So studied was their determination to be calm and natural with each other that Roger had congratulated himself on the mature wisdom of his move.

Rebecca watched them like hawks. Their civility made her suspicious. Across the flickering glow of the camp fire she watched them exchange cautious signals. Roger's jovial ignorance bothered her. She did not understand her mother's coyness, but she felt angry about it. David, she reasoned, was capable of anything. She lay low and observed.

Their laughter, at first stilted and forced, had become easier, loosened by the floating haze of alcohol and mindless chitchat.

"They are weird," Jason whispered to his sister. "Do you want a drink?"

She looked at him accusingly as he pulled out a thermos from under the blanket. He smelled like smoke and brine, the pungent perfume of evenings at the beach.

"These are ours," he whispered. "I made 'em this afternoon."

It annoyed her on principle that she did not know about his secret bartending. Rebecca prided herself on her uncanny skills of nosing around, figuring things out. The idea that he could pull something off without her knowledge scalded her.

They were laughing loudly now, as round four of margaritas was poured. Her mother's shrill giggle embarrassed her. The wood hissed and spat flying embers, like hostile fireworks aiming at an airborne target.

"Pass me a Dixie cup, please."

Roger handed her the package, not pausing to interrupt a funny story he'd told a hundred times.

"Fill this fucker up," she said to her brother.

"All right!" he enthused.

It occurred to Samantha that the kids were unusually quiet, but she was too preoccupied with her own anxious stirrings to pursue it further. When he wasn't looking she studied him in the firelight.

The grotesque distortions from the shadow of the flames stretched his face in all directions. Still, he was a handsome man, she concluded. Darker, more mysterious than Roger. Her eyes moved to the blond storyteller gesticulating wildly. His biceps rippled under the summer moon, and she recalled how she had fixated on his muscular arms the first time they had made love. The hump of his bicep formed a pillow for her neck when he'd slide his arm under her head.

She had been so glad to be there.

For some reason, the image of his arms had stayed with her.

David's arms were rather thin and nondescript. When he would enfold her in them, they felt like rough and fragile rope. He had no muscle to speak of; the bones of his elbows hurt her in bed with their pointy jabs.

She had sighed and moaned unmercifully in those skinny tendrils.

She looked back at the culprit, who caught her, and she quickly stared back into the fire.

Rebecca witnessed it all.

"They really make me sick," she whispered to her brother, who refilled her Dixie cup and agreed with her, for different reasons.

They had moved on to the stranger-than-fiction aspects of their individual professions.

David related amusing anecdotes of dotty colleagues whose misguided research had become well-known theories, studied and revered as higher truths from lofty institutions. He recounted with great panache the countless examples of misquoted messages, misinterpreted passages of scanty criticism that had gone on to become yardsticks of excellence toward which overly enthusiastic scholars would bow and genuflect.

Rebecca listened to this dissertation with cynical enthusiasm. She wanted to ask him where he fit in— making phony research or perpetuating the lies to others.

"More," she whispered to her brother, who obliged by filling her cup to the brim.

It was Sam's turn next. She told them about Roland, the union struggles, and their resourcefulness at putting things together creatively so the show could go on. She described the fiasco of a couple of years ago, when everyone was on strike just before a sold-out production of *Glass Menagerie* had been slated to preview. She and Roland had rampaged through the apartments, homes, and garages of everyone they'd ever known. Even people on vacation got robbed by them, all sense of fair play abandoned in their frantic search.

And they had made it. By opening night an entire living room set had been assembled from purloined bits and pieces slapped together. Only one minor oversight proved their undoing.

They had needed a tape deck for music in the scene when Jim asks Laura to dance after the Blue Roses speech, when the strains of a waltz drift in from the Paradise Dance Hall. She'd snatched Jason's, but forgot to note there was a tape already in place, and in the chaos and excitement never got around to tracking down appropriate music. So instead of a waltz resembling "La Golondrina," the screeching wails of Metallica had filled the theater, sending the actors into stupefaction and the audience into peals of laughter.

She was aware of underscoring her own role in this tale, elaborating to make it sound extremely important—though it was important, and her resourcefulness most ingenious. She wanted them both to see that.

They laughed and hooted the chamber music of the solidly intoxicated. She could feel the numbing effects of the tequila and allowed herself to be blanketed by its hazy cushion. Now that she thought about it, the circumstances of this evening struck her funny.

Roger swaggered to his feet. David stared at him through anesthetized eyes, wondering what an insurance man could possibly contribute to the world's absurdity except himself.

He stole a glance at Samantha to see if he could find passion in her eyes for this ordinary man who sold premiums and policies. She caught his eye in the amber firelight and smiled in tender recognition.

Rebecca saw it all.

"One time I was sent up to Modesto to check out this agricultural company that wanted coverage against fire and theft."

He is tedious, but a kindly sort, David assured himself.

"Turns out it's a buncha guys jerkin' off cows."

Both children set down their cups and tuned in.

"No shit, it's a bull semen ranch. They sell the stuff for four thousand bucks a unit."

Sam stared at this curious stranger; she'd never heard this tale before.

"This guy takes me on a tour, and I can't fucking believe it! He goes to a supply room and takes out this big plastic vagina and a tube of K-Y jelly."

"What's K-Y jelly?" Jason whispered to his sister, who drunkenly promised to tell him later.

Sam had forgotten about the kids, or she would have cautioned Roger to launder his language.

"Big scrotums are where it's at—he tells me this, right?—and he takes me into a room where a buncha bulls have been led by the nose to a group of queer steers (that's the bovine equivalent of a whore), and he tells me to watch while he humps and dumps."

David rolled on the blanket in laughter while Samantha held her arms close to her body, convulsed. The children were stony silent, except for Jason's occasional murmur of "This is insane."

"So this gigantic steer rears up and starts moving—I mean, moving! His thing looks like a fuckin' pogo stick. This guy slides the 'A.V.,' as they call it, under the bull, and the guy jerks him off and sells the stuff to Japan."

"You're joking!" David plied him with hilarity.

"No way José. Eleven fuckin' million dollars in foreign sales last year."

"How do they advertise it, 'Jizz for Biz'?" David choked out between chuckles.

"What's jizz?" Jason whispered, trying to follow.

"Later," she hissed back, enthralled and only mildly disgusted. It amused her to hear adults talk dirty, especially Roger, who purported to dislike what he called bad language.

"They've got a goddamn magazine, a picture magazine for cows! No shit! *Sires on Parade*—I saw it, my hand before God."

"God's dead," Rebecca chimed in unexpectedly, but no one heard her except David, who mumbled across the flames, "That's just what we need; an existentialist in the crowd."

"What did he say?" Jason asked.

"Nothing," Rebeccca replied, and filled her own cup this time.

She stared directly into David's eyes. There was no question in her mind. Quickly she looked to her mother, who was still enthralled by Roger's transformation into an off-color raconteur.

"He shows me these steers whose dicks have been

fixed to fly off at a thirty-degree angle. They're used to sniff out the horny women cows."

"That's disgusting!" Rebecca yelled into the ocean breeze.

"Hell, they've got hormones to make 'em horny at the rancher's convenience."

"Sickening! Shades of Orwell, not to mention revolting!"

Roger pirouetted to face his daughter, sitting Indian style on the blanket, a judgmental squaw at the tribal meeting.

"For your information, John Lennon and his wife were investors."

"Far fuckin' out!' shrieked Jason from the background.

"I think it's sick."

"Why? They had to shelter their money in something; might as well have been in bulls' balls."

The adults snickered with delight; everyone did, except Rebecca, who rose to her feet woozy and a little cold.

"I think you guys are weirder than shit."

Samantha focused on her swaying daughter.

"Roger, she's been drinking. Where's Jason?"

They scrambled for a second, each in his stumbling manner, trying to locate the boy, who had passed out on the blanket.

"He's drunk as a skunk!" Roger uttered, unable to contain his amused surprise.

Rebecca screamed into the salty air.

"How can you be so stupid!"

Roger turned toward her, genuinely surprised at her sudden outburst.

"Are you talking to me, Rebecca, or do you mean all

of us?" He made a grand gesture, sweeping the group around the fire. Sam and David exchanged a quick regard of alarm.

"Look at those two." She pointed her accusatory finger in the direction of her mother. Roger followed with his eyes, aware that he had drunk far too much. David and Sam looked like oddly paired dominoes, their silhouettes distorted by the dancing shadows of the fire.

"You're so dumb, Roger," Rebecca hissed in an inebriated stage whisper.

"Those two are in love, and you can't even see it! They're practically doing it under your nose, and you're telling jokes."

Roger tried to absorb the impact of Rebecca's testimony, but he couldn't quite bring himself to go over it bit by bit. Instead he simply turned to Sam and asked her, "Are you sleeping with him?"

"What do you need, a map?" Rebecca spat out, before her mother could answer. Roger flailed his hand in a hush-hush signal, as if silence were mandatory while he carefully re-posed the question.

"Sam," he inquired calmly, "have you gone to bed with him—here, now in L.A.?" He labored to get the precise details in place.

"Yes," she responded, surprising herself with how easy it was to simply tell the truth. It occurred to her that she had no desire to explain it further.

No one could have predicted the rage that came so suddenly. Roger, not a man given to tirades and tantrums, had within seconds escalated his voice to a thunderous roar.

"You lying, betraying shit! You set this whole thing up!"

"That's not so," interrupted Sam, wishing her head were not so fogged with alcohol.

"Shut the fuck up!" he yelled at her. "What kind of an absolute fool do you take me for? Is it too much to ask that my wife stay out of bed with the guy who wrecked her life in the first place?"

"Roger, that's not what happened. You don't understand."

"What's to understand? A cheating slut is a cheating slut! *I'm* your fucking husband, not him."

He kicked an avalanche of sand in their direction. Rebecca cried silently, mostly from fear. Jason was still asleep.

"I know you're my husband, Roger," Sam said emphatically.

"Shut up, whore; I should have known you wouldn't keep away from him."

David considered speaking up, but the man's fury seemed genuinely out of control.

"Roger, don't call me names. What happened has nothing to do with us."

Roger came at her, and Sam jumped to her feet. David vaulted to protect her lest Roger take a swing. Instead, he grabbed her arm and pressed his fingers into her flesh.

"Goddamn it, Samantha, you belong to *me*!" he screamed.

"I belong to myself!" she yelled at the top of her lungs, and tried to shake free of his grasp. David moved forward.

"Now see here, man, let's be reasonable."

Roger swung around with all his might. "You son of a bitch!" he hissed, and slugged him squarely in the jaw. David hit the sand with a resounding thud. Roger dove on top of him, punching and pounding, while Sam tugged and screamed for them to stop.

Rebecca cried out loud and moved in to help her mother. Jason woke up with a start and threw up.

With a force she did not know she possessed, Samantha shoved Roger off David and shrieked at them to stop.

"It's time for you to go home, David," she announced to the bloody face on the sand. "Now just go!"

Roger stood behind her, panting, his fist still gnarled and ready in hard knots.

"Let's get the stuff, Roger. Rebecca, help us bring our things up to the house. The party's over. I hope you're satisfied," she spat at her sobbing daughter. She didn't give her time to answer.

22

She decided to put the children to bed before she dealt with any of it. The liquor had worn off, and she could feel the dull throb of a headache starting at the base of her neck. A sour, bilious taste hung in her mouth. Jason had vomited all over her sweatshirt, which reeked of margarita mix and onion dip. She and Roger peeled off his foul-smelling clothes and rinsed him off in the shower, where he threw up again. Fumes of malodorous steam wafted up from the pool of light green liquid being splattered and splayed by the force of the shower.

Roger toweled him off while Sam went to tend to Rebecca.

She was huddled in a corner of her bed, crouched in a ball and crying. She smelled of smoldering embers and salty air.

"I'm sorry, Mom."

"Forget it," Sam snapped. "Put on your pajamas and get into bed."

Rebecca sobbed as if her heart would break.

"I didn't mean to wreck everything."

"You didn't wreck everything."

"Mom?" Rebecca asked, hesitantly testing the water.

"What?" Sam sighed. She was tired.

"You told me you loved Roger."

"I do love Roger."

"But what about David?"

"I told you, I love Roger. What happened with David is no one's business. It has nothing to do with our lives."

Rebecca listened to her mother's sharp tone and started to cry again.

"I'm sorry I hurt you," she said, meaning it.

Sam stopped for a second and drew a deep breath. She reached out her hand and brushed Rebecca's hair out of her face. "Love is terribly complicated sometimes. Good night, sweetie."

She walked into her bedroom and closed the door. Roger was already in bed, sulking and hurt. She slid out of her clothes and quickly showered. Out of the corner of her eye she noticed he had not changed position.

It is true, she told herself. I do love Roger. He looks painfully vulnerable sitting there, she marked guiltily.

Samantha slipped into her nightie and sat down on the edge of the bed. Gently she put her hand on his leg. He shoved it away in one hostile gesture.

"If that's your idea of an apology . . ."

"That wasn't an apology, Roger. I can't say I'm sorry when I'm not."

Roger threw back the covers and bolted to his feet.

"You . . . you—Christ, it's not enough that you cheat

on me, now you want to give me speeches. Fuck you, Samantha."

"Stop it, Roger. You're acting like a possessive adolescent."

"You're my goddamn wife!"

"And I was once *his* goddamn wife."

"Does that mean you get carte blanche to screw him?"

She tried to restrain the sudden surge of pity she felt for him, the desire to protect him and shield him from the hurt of the moment. A wave of icy lucidity swept over her as she realized how vital it was at this moment to tell the absolute truth, and to do it as cleanly, as clearly, as was ever in her life possible. Anything said carelessly, vaguely, would inextricably alter the terrain of their marriage. The slightest nuance, the barest innuendo of denial, would create a space for deception that could be used again and again when the need for murky secrets arose, a storage closet where raw truths could be safely sequestered from view.

"I don't expect you to understand this, Roger, but I'm going to tell you the truth. We slept together to kill off love."

"What do I look like, a jerk? I don't buy it, Sam."

"It doesn't matter what you buy; it's the truth. I don't love David, Roger. I love you."

"You have some pretty questionable ways of showing it."

"You're not my judge, Roger. You do not own the rights to my life."

"I have some rights here—son of a bitch!" He kicked the mattress as if he were aiming for a field goal. His childishness annoyed her, and she bolted to her feet and kicked at it from her side.

"Listen to me, just listen—and I mean it!"

He sat on the side of the bed, amazed at this sudden show of fury. It was his place to be enraged, not hers.

"Roger, I had a life before I met you! A complete life! A job, a husband, children, love, hate, problems, the lot. I have a whole history that doesn't include you. That's fact. I can't change it."

"I'm not asking you to."

"Yes you are! In essence you're telling me to erase that life. I can't! David and I had a life together, Roger, and there was love. How can I tell you there wasn't? This isn't our first marriage. I can't change the past for you, Roger, although God knows I would, sometimes."

He didn't say anything; there was nothing he could offer for the moment.

"Don't you think I wonder about you and Suzy? Sometimes when our life is filled with boring routine and mere functioning, I think about what you must have been like together. Young, carefree, beautiful, childless. I wasn't those things, Roger, I wasn't any of them. I came to you as a bitter divorcée trailing two kids, no money, and a pile of problems I saw as unsolvable."

He smiled ever so slightly, remembering that fateful day in Saperstein's office.

"But I wasn't always like that. I was young and passionate. I was childless and in love with art and David Bartholomew. When he left, there was no closing, just loose, frazzled, hurtful ends. Those are over now. We fucked them away, dead, gone. Can you in any way understand that?"

"No. I hate your past with him."

"And I hate yours! But she's dead, so you can afford to be smug!"

He let that digest for a bit; indeed, until recently he had never even fantasized Suzy in relation to his life with Samantha. There was no link, no connection; he couldn't honestly remember what he was like in those days. When he reflected on the past, it inevitably recalled the ocean and the sun all tied up in a haze of souvenirs.

"My life with you means the world to me, Roger."

"I wish I could believe that," Roger snapped.

"You're going to have to have faith in us."

Roger pondered that for a bit. How could he have faith in a woman who had betrayed him with a man he considered detestable?

"I want that son of a bitch out of our lives—totally," he pronounced authoritatively.

"He is still the children's father."

"Some fucking father. I'm the real 'father.' "

"In that sense, you're right, Roger."

"Then cancel this last Sunday."

"I can't do that. He has a right to see them."

"That bastard takes great liberties with his rights. Cancel it for me, Sam, for us."

"I can't do that. I'm sorry."

She watched the anger in his face fade into disappointment, a transition she'd memorized from her children's continual equations of If you really loved me, you would. She held her ground.

"It will do us good to be alone for the weekend, Roger."

"I don't like it at all, Sam."

"I can't ask you to like it any more than I could say he can't see the children."

"I still don't like it," he announced matter-of-factly.

"I don't love David, Roger; I'm sure of that now."

He just looked at her blankly, feeling neither happy nor comforted by this revelation.

"Let's go to sleep," Sam whispered, and reached over to turn out the light.

23

"I don't care what you say, I'm not about to check into a hotel with that man!"

"Rebecca, that man is your father. Besides, Jason will be there too."

"That's worse! You said only Sundays; now it's a weekend, next it'll be custody. Forget it!"

"Aw, man, can't I just go by myself? She's *such* a jerk," Jason wailed.

"Don't call your sister names, and no, you can't."

"It's fine by me," Rebecca sneered, and shoved her brother away from her private territory at the table.

"Hey, doggy, we had a radical time without you before. Even he said it was better."

"What did he say, Jason?" Samantha asked. Her voice tottered close to the defensive.

She had hoped this time would be different, more

equitable for her daughter. All the men in her life had been partial to Jason, and although she understood precisely why that happened, still it pained her. She had hoped that Rebecca's father would see her differently, appreciate those things that were bright and fine in her, buried treasure under layers of moldy, sodden hatefulness packed in tightly from so many years of being scarcely tolerated and compared with a brother who was uncomplicatedly adored.

"He said it was easier when she wasn't around."

"Well, be that as it may, he was nice enough to offer you kids a weekend in San Diego. I know you'll have a good time, there's so much to see."

"Yeah, I really want to see some asshole whale brush his teeth."

"Aw, man, can she stay here?"

"Absolutely not."

"Why?" both of them demanded in unison.

"Because it's your last visit with him, and you'll have a good time."

Not all of her reasons brimmed with altruism. She and Roger were looking forward to a weekend alone, without the tensions of fighting children and compromising schedules.

Both of them wanted to be free of the weight of David's presence, yet neither spoke of it to the other. Roger planned to woo her back, entice her into the safe and solid security of the rhythm of their lives. Sam anticipated relaxing from the jangled divisiveness of the last month. She knew that little by little she would ease back into the armored loveliness of a marriage she had chosen and helped to build.

They needed this time together. And they intended to have it.

And oddly enough, the object of their restless up-heaval had provided the opportunity.

"I'm not going!" Rebecca insisted.

"Oh, yes you are," Sam said, and meant it.

She helped them pack amidst wails and protests that did not move her at all.

"You can go and see the Globe's new theater."

"I hate new buildings."

"Then you can go to the museums in Balboa Park."

"Natural history gags me."

"There's Sea World."

"Dancing dolphins? Don't bore me to death."

"Well, you're going, and that's that."

"What if he tries things on me in the hotel?"

"That'll be the day, scuz bag. He's not that desper-ate."

"Both of you stop this instant!"

"She's trying to get rid of us," Rebecca informed her brother.

"You're absolutely correct," Sam reassured her, with a resonant click of the suitcase.

"Well, I'm not going to have a good time."

"That's his problem, not mine."

He came in for a cup of coffee, and they chatted about nothing specific. She remarked that he looked rested in the morning sunlight. Roger was out on a claim, but he promised to return early. For no earthly reason, she wanted to ask David if he still loved her.

"Yea, dude," Jason sang, and bounced into the kitchen with his skateboard tucked under his arm.

"Dragon Lady's almost ready. Can we stay in a hotel with a good TV? There's some good stuff on tonight."

"I'm sure that can be arranged."

"Bitchin', dude."

"What?"

"That's bad."

"Bad means good, David. You'll catch on after a bit."

"Right, and you can talk as stupidly as he does."

"Good morning, Rebecca."

"Sure thing," she sneered at him, and plunked her backpack down on the floor.

"I'm being coerced into this against my will!" she accused, looking toward her mother for further proof.

"Oh?"

"We can always leave her in the car, like most people do with their dogs," Jason added.

"Knock it off, both of you. They're all yours, David. Consider keeping them forever."

He'd already fantasized about that in his moments of fancying himself the quintessential father—handsome, capable, creatively raising two children alone in Boston. He'd be stacks of fun as a parent, leading them to museums, plays, concerts, and lectures. His colleagues at work would fall all over themselves with sympathetic understanding, offering to sub his classes when he was obligated to take them to the dentist or to their lessons.

His girlfriends would understand and love him all the more for his capacity to extend himself to his children.

Taking on these kids was out of the question.

At least full time. He wouldn't survive it.

"You're not taking your skateboard, are you? How embarrassing."

"For whom?" David inquired honestly.

"Just wait," Rebecca warned him.

He didn't know exactly for what he ought to wait.

"Everybody ready?"

"Willing and able," Rebecca scoffed, dragging her backpack along and creating deep grooves in the carpet that looked like gashes.

"I'll call and let you know where we're staying."

"You mean you don't already have a hotel? Mom, I'll probably have to sleep on the beach."

"You'll survive," Sam told her daughter, who was already huffing her way down the stairs. Jason was skateboarding in the driveway; he maneuvered a perfect 360.

"Have a good time, David."

She smiled at him with the sad knowledge that he would try to, and if things went as planned, it would be a moderately pleasant weekend.

"Bye," he said, and without thinking leaned his face down toward hers and kissed her lightly and sweetly on the mouth.

"Sunday," he murmured almost inaudibly, and made his way toward the car.

Sam closed the door softly. She could smell his scent on her face. The sweetness of talc and the bitterness of tobacco.

Rebecca had claimed the front seat. She hovered by the door and extracted three thick volumes from her backpack. He watched her from the corner of his eye. At this angle he could not decipher the titles, and he didn't recognize the covers.

Jason was singing in the backseat. Something about good thing where have you gone. He didn't have a bad voice, though it was obviously rudimentary and untrained.

He studied the plethora of green-and-white billboards indicating directions. He veered the car to the lane on the right, hoping like hell that this tributary led to San Diego.

"What are you reading?"

"A book."

"I can see that," he sighed. Clearly, she was out to sabotage this weekend. He prepared himself for the onslaught of acrimony she would pelt him with until he would get fed up and lecture her, after which she would enter into her sulk.

In four days he would be in Boston.

The thought sustained him.

Elizabeth would pick him up at Logan, and he would instruct her to drive directly to Faneuil Hall, where he would detail everything to her over vodka and Bulgarian caviar. She would fill him in on every innuendo of the in-house battles of the literature department, every tidbit of who was sleeping with whom, and why. He relished these reunions. Elizabeth was a true friend, the kind he would have liked to have had in Samantha years ago. But Samantha was his love.

Elizabeth was clearly not. Any sexuality between them now would be redundant, a step backward, even. He didn't want that to happen; he valued her too much to allow it.

"I brought three large books so I wouldn't be bored to death."

"Aw, man, are we gonna have to listen to this?"

"No," Rebecca snapped. "I intend to be completely out of the way. You two can have your good time alone like you want."

"Radical!"

"What do you mean, Rebecca?"

"Listen, Jason already told me that you preferred to be with him, like the night he ran away."

"Well, you did say that," Jason wailed, as David shot him a dirty look.

"Well, it's all the same to me," Rebecca sniffed. "I don't want to be with you any more than you want to be with me. So it's a truce. You two do your number and just let me read."

"I did not say that, Rebecca."

"It doesn't matter."

"Sure it matters. What I said was, it's easier when you two are not fighting."

"Sure."

"That's exactly what I meant, anyway."

Jason sat silently in the backseat. For the first time he felt slightly uneasy with his father.

"I was sort of hoping that you and I could steal a little time together and talk about books."

"We'll see," she replied suspiciously, just a little bit delighted.

24

The brochure promised a total concept in family vacationing. He'd assumed it was like the Concord in the Catskills, where every petty whim was catered to, if his memory served.

When David was eleven years old, the congregation of Saint Andrew's had rented a bus and a string of rooms at that grand resort in upstate New York so that the less-than-affluent parishioners could have a summer holiday away from the tedium of Pittsfield. Nellie and David packed their bags with excitement and anticipation. As the bus crossed the state line west of Massachusetts, David gazed at the landscape of what he assumed would be foreign territory. Nellie had warned him of the dangers of polio contracted from unchlorinated water and suspicious drinking fountains. David had brought along a stack of books, on the outside chance he would find no companions his age, since the idea of playing sports alone intimidated him.

The church matrons oohed and aahed at the large edifice amid the trees that offered swimming pools, miniature golf courses, shuffleboard courts, and wooden dance floors. Their room was called a suite, which meant three beds were cramped into the space.

His mother and her friends flocked to the cake-decorating classes and the flower-arrangement get-togethers. David roamed the grounds, disappointed in the crowds of people who appeared to be amused by horseshoes and the sandlot scores of father-son duets playing stickball or relay races. The sight of their uncomplicated joy pained him so much that he sequestered himself in his room to read. He was not accustomed to these kinds of people, who dressed up in suits and furs, despite the oppressive stillness of the evening, to go and hear a second-rate comedian deliver his tired one-liners to the smoke-filled hall that served as a cafeteria by day.

"You're not having a good time, are you, David?" Nellie asked sadly.

"It's okay," he confessed, softening his revulsion at the entire affair.

"We paid good money to come here," Nellie pushed.

"I know," David admitted guiltily.

"Then try and have a good time."

He assured her he would, and dragged himself to meals served family style in the large dining hall, where people scooped up disgraceful amounts of macaroni-and-cheese, of jello and meat loaf. He didn't go to the bingo games or the evening dances, but retreated to his room to pray for forgiveness for not honoring his father or mother. He questioned his mute Savior as to how to honor a father who didn't exist, but no answer came to him.

Even during his wildest infidelities years later, he avoided any hotel with reference to family accommodations. Somehow, passion and children could not be housed under the same roof.

When the pretty young clerk at Visitor Information had suggested Vacation Village, he'd recoiled in horror; even the pamphlet annoyed him.

"It's the only place left with space, sir."

That word again.

"Why?" he inquired, surprised at his own abruptness.

"Because it's the Beach Volley Ball Tournament."

"And what may that be?"

She regarded him as an arrogant oddity, probably from some remote place like Butte, Montana, or Moscow, Idaho, where people think of California as a terrain for earthquakes, mass murderers, and tropical rain showers.

"It's kinda hard to explain. It's like baseball at the beach."

"Oh."

"I would strongly suggest that you take a drive over to Vacation Village. They'll be full by two o'clock."

He thanked her politely and then rescued Jason from the parking lot, where he and his skateboard careened around in fairly impressive turn slides, hand plants, and half-twists.

Rebecca slouched in the front seat and read *A Tree Grows in Brooklyn*. It surprised him that she had picked that one. He would not have guessed her inclinations to be that sentimental.

"Let's go!" he yelled to Jason, who bunny-hopped his board all the way to the rented car.

*   *   *

They had made love in the living room before lunch. Roger tackled her as soon as he got home, letting out a *Yahoo!* and a *Yippee!* that set them both at ease.

He sang a battered rendition of Richie Havens's "Freedom" as he tore off her T-shirt and jeans. They had laughed together afterward, and it had felt good and made them hungry, so they stumbled into the kitchen half-clothed and made greasy omelets and guacamole.

"I want to rent every trashy movie in L.A."

"Who gets to decide what's trash?"

"I do," she smirked, as a hunk of cooked egg slipped accidentally from the corner of her mouth.

"I wonder how the kids are doing," Roger considered neutrally.

"My sympathies are with David today."

"Is that so?" he teased, shoving the tinge of aggression to the back of his throat.

"They were awful this morning. Rebecca screamed and yelled, told him she was coerced into being with him."

"In a sense that's true. Maybe we should have let her stay home."

"Are you kidding?"

"Not completely."

"We have two full days alone," she reminded him, her voice rising slightly with impatience.

"That's true. Still, maybe she's not comfortable with him."

"I don't believe this," Sam said incredulously, aware that the roots of anger were growing in her stomach. "He's almost out of here, we get a vacation, and you're worried about Rebecca being comfortable."

"I was only voicing a concern about my daughter, my daughter, his daughter—Christ!"

"Roger?"

"Hm?"

"Are we all right here?"

"I think so," he sighed, and tried to sound convincing.

It wasn't so terrible. Neatly rowed cabanas lined the bay side, where gentle breezes barely stirred the carefully manicured lawns surrounding the hotel. Discreet signs indicated directions to such destinations as the Barefoot Bar, the Tiki Room, and the outdoor courts and pool.

Jason had raced to verify that the color television came in loud and clear.

Rebecca put her things neatly where they belonged and took her book out on the grassy slope by the bay.

David got his own things arranged and walked out to join his daughter.

"I read that book."

"So," she sniffed, looking back at the page.

"So I liked it, and I thought Aunt Sissy was one terrific character."

"Why?" He had piqued her interest here; she loved Aunt Sissy.

"Because she steals Bibles and rubbers and she sort of says what's on her mind. And she's funny."

"I'm not laughing."

"Perhaps you're not far enough along in the book."

"We'll see."

"Do you like Frannie?"

"She's all right."

"I love her."

"Why?"

"Because she's bright and resourceful, and her mother favors her brother."

"Hm."

"I have a penchant for underdogs. The unwashed, the unloved, etcetera."

"I'll just bet," Rebecca scoffed, returning to her book.

"I meant what I said about Frannie; I love her. She's the most worthwhile person in the book."

"Yeah; it's too bad her father was a drunk who died and left her."

"Her father was a pitiful creature, actually."

"Yeah, yeah, I've got to have compassion for him. You don't need to say it again."

"I had no intention of saying it."

"Well, I do feel sorry for him. But I feel sorry for her, too."

They were silent for a moment, letting the hollow slap of tiny waves hit against the flat sand of the bay.

"Your brother wants to go to Sea World."

"So take him."

"I'd prefer that you came with us."

"That kind of attraction gags me, if you want to know the truth."

"Me, too, as long as we're being honest. Caged mammals are grotesque, when you think about it."

"Then why do you want to go there?"

"I don't. Jason does."

"Do you always do what others want?"

He laughed at this one. She didn't see her question as amusing. Suspecting she'd been mocked by him, she slid her face back into the safe folds of the book.

"I'm not laughing at you, goddamn it! What you said is sadly droll."

"Don't use big words to cover up."

"Rebecca, I *never* do what others want; can't you see how funny that is? I'm trying to learn to bend a little."

"I see your point."

"Will you please join us?"

She shrugged her shoulders and looked out at the Hobie Cats swiftly sliding across the smooth surface of the bay. A colorful barrage of sails slithered around like seafaring kites dancing around the water.

Apparently, some kind of regatta was in progress. In any case, it was beautiful there under the shade of palm trees swaying to the restrained rhythm of a temperate breeze. Every element seemed in harmony with the next. If this had been a movie set, he pondered to himself, the actors would have to mesh into the awesome tranquility of the location.

He considered himself sadly miscast, sitting here with a child who didn't like him, cajoling her to accompany him to a place he couldn't fathom.

He thought about Boston, the impossibly noisy streets crowded with fast walkers who shoved past you without saying Excuse me, the filthy subway stations smelling of smoke and urine and steam, the distressing honk of the taxi demanding the right-of-way, and ill-tempered bus drivers determined not to give it to them.

He couldn't wait to get home.

"Come on. We can secretly laugh at everybody."

"I thought people were supposed to be sad, not funny."

"Rebecca," he said, losing patience. "Do you or do you not choose to accompany me? I would like it if you did, but I'm not about to sit here and supplicate you."

"Why do you want me along?"

"Because, believe it or not, I rather like your company."

"Well, I don't believe it," she sniffed and rolled over, "but I'll go."

25

Roland had suggested *The Rose.* "The Divine Miss M. has never been more celestial than in this one, petal. Besides, you said you wanted a little trash."

Samantha hadn't closely followed Bette Midler's career, but she'd always liked the performer's manic verve and offbeat melodies. And *The Rose* was one of the many films that had slipped by her during those years consumed with the basics of coping and child care.

Roger had been a fan of Janis Joplin's. He possessed every one of her records and had once traveled north to catch her performance at the Monterey Pop Festival. He never approved much of the hippie counterculture, and he most certainly did not approve of drugs, but he was drawn to the blues sung by Janis.

Her music moved him. And he frequently longed to be moved.

Sam had always liked Joplin's musical performances, especially when she talked and teased the audience, pulling painful "Yeah, baby"'s from them as she seared their hearts with tales of mistreatment, heartache, loss. Manipulating them into a heated frenzy, she'd tug one last admission of shared sadness from them and then burst into a shrieking rendition of "Cry, Baby," and she had them begging for more.

David used to refer to her as a cultural metaphor of the '60s, living proof that flower children had created an arena where unattractive girls could flourish, even shine. He pointed out Joplin's need for outrageous costumes— feather and finery of self-decoration—with a bottle of Southern Comfort always at her side to enhance her tragic persona.

"You're full of shit," she had reminded him, with increasing annoyance. She loved the rebellion of Janis, her foul mouth and her squeaky undertones of rage. Sam fancied her a female version of James Dean, all swagger and torchy indifference. Sam had always suspected he resented the intrusion of Janis Joplin on what he regarded as his personal terrain of suffering.

Better Midler was terrific as Joplin. She strutted and fretted her hour upon the stage in offbeat dresses, a floppy mop of uncombed corkscrews, runny noses and melting mascara, and her creaky, croaky, blues-belting voice.

They wolfed down strawberry bonbons and loved every minute of it.

He wasn't expecting such large crowds at the marine attraction. It took him a full ten minutes to find a parking spot. He'd been shamefully tempted to snag one of the spaces reserved for the handicapped, but pride had forbidden it—as well as his children, who would stalk his callousness like night prowlers and request he go elsewhere.

Despite both of their protests, Jason had insisted on toting his skateboard.

"Aw, man, what's it to you?"

Perhaps he had a point, though David felt hard pressed to decipher it. He'd considered putting his foot down, taking a stand and saying no, but he suspected he would need his arsenal of authoritative vetoes for more important issues.

His son wove in and out of the parked cars like a slalom skier caught in a downhill race.

"Just pretend you don't know him," Rebecca suggested.

"Good idea," he agreed. "It's one of the benefits of not looking alike. I can ignore him totally."

He paid for their tickets at a booth constructed to look like a tiki hut. The girl handed him a map and a schedule of spectacles where the time and location were spelled out in large block letters.

Clusters of people snaked their way through what was designed to look like a tropical paradise divided by asphalt footpaths. Rebecca ambled along, taking it all in slowly, cautiously.

"This is disgusting," she whispered to her father. He agreed with her.

Jason hung ten down an incline, scooted down to a hand plant, and executed a perfect slide turn.

A young fellow dressed like a sailor from *Mutiny on the Bounty* except that he carried a broom and dustpan with him approached Jason immediately.

"You're gonna have to give that over, son."

"What?"

"Signs are posted everywhere. No skateboarding. I'll check it into the Lost and Found, and you can claim it as you leave."

Jason turned to his father for assistance, but David and Rebecca had wandered off to look at the baby seals swimming contentedly in an open-air pond.

He gave it to the guy reluctantly in exchange for a claim ticket.

He didn't tell them about it, and they didn't notice.

"I suggest we hit the underwater ballet as our first attraction. We might luck out and witness some recent defectors working off-season to make ends meet."

Rebecca smiled a little and stood in the line leading toward a sunken theater. The tiny jingle of a bell signaled them that they could enter the covered amphitheater with an enormous tank as the stage. A young girl in a nautical dress waved a flashlight to direct the incoming traffic of humanity into orderly rows. The crescent of plastic bleachers filled up rapidly, and the house lights dimmed on cue.

From a loudspeaker somewhere out of view, a rich and resonant voice welcomed them to Sea World's underwater gala and began a story of medieval intrigue. As each character was introduced, a springy gray dolphin would dive into the tank and circle the bottom at an impressive speed.

The hidden raconteur continued his tale of damsels in distress, and soon the tank was teeming with dressed-up dolphins and pretty mermaids lowered on swings with masks and tanks discreetly attached to their sleek, svelte bodies. Blond and brunette tresses swayed like sargasso plants in gentle seas.

To the strains of a Viennese waltz the ladies hooked

up to the dolphins, and they all sashayed around the bowl.

"The brunette in the corner is Margot Fonteyn," Rebecca whispered in her father's ear.

"Then who's the blonde on the other side?"

"A contestant from 'Star Search.'"

He reminded himself to ask Jason what that meant.

They were all turning somersaults by now, graceful turns, the weightless buoyancy of underwater.

"Did you know that dolphins are capable of love?" Rebecca inquired softly.

He didn't, but he was delighted she retained such information.

People applauded the empty tank and now silent loudspeaker. The flashlight lady announced the next hour's worth of spectacles, winding up with an enthusiastic endorsement of the park's pride and joy.

"Shamu goes to college!" she yelled into the amphitheater, and some of the audience clapped with delight.

Jason was one of them.

"I certainly hope it's an Ivy League school," David clucked as they filed out the door.

"I wonder how he did on his SATs," Rebecca remarked.

"Killer whales don't have to do well on anything," David mused.

This show was in an open-air amphitheater, where the sun beat down its mercilessly hot waves. Several people had folded their programs into makeshift hats as protection from the rays. They looked like play soldiers sitting there in their newsprint helmets.

A row of children in wheelchairs caught David's eye. He figured it must be an outing of some kind, since there

were so many of them. He studied their cheerful demeanor, and the faces of whom he guessed to be the
mothers. He wanted to find the looks of rage, betrayal,
the angry resignation etched in the curve of a lip, the set
of a jaw.

He could find neither.

The children howled and hollered like any others,
stretching to sock their neighbors good-naturedly on the
arms, moving only the upper torso, as if the rest had been
dismissed as useless and simply ignored.

The loudspeaker announced the arrival of its fierce
baline, and Shamu swam out to greet the guests. He was
an enormous hunk of black-and-white flesh, so massive
indeed that David was stupefied. His proximity to sea
mammals had been limited to the sanctity and safety of
the pages of *Moby Dick*.

The audience went crazy.

He stared at the children in the steel chairs below
him. They applauded wildly, shrieking excitement into
the scorching, arid air. One little girl moved a bit too far
forward and started to fall. He gasped audibly as he
watched the child's mother swiftly and gently shove her
back into the seat.

It occurred to him that he should be grateful for
having normal children.

And it occurred to him that this was the first time
he'd entertained such a thought.

He pondered the magnitude of that while the killer
whale balanced books on his snout, sported huge horn-
rimmed spectacles, and jumped through hoops held high
in the air by a man he guessed to be the trainer.

A microphone was placed next to the whale's mouth.
His buccal cavity looked like a depthless cavern lined
with rows of ominous-looking teeth.

He thought about Jonah and Pinocchio. He tried to imagine the interior of a whale's belly.

A suffocating pink-and-blue chamber of slimy flesh held up by massive ribs and vertebrae. The very idea sent shivers down his spine.

"This is pathetic," Rebecca hissed. "I don't see why the SPCA doesn't come down on them."

Jason looked at her with a sneer and rolled his eyes in a flutter of impatience.

The crowds clapped wildly for an encore, and Shamu obliged them by cruising around the pool a couple more times and taking one valiant leap that caused a geyser of water to shoot up and soak the crowd seated in the front row.

"Have you noticed," Rebecca groused, "that even in an animal show, the bright ones are always made to look like geeks?"

"Well . . ." Jason sniffed.

"I wasn't talking to you."

Jason got a jump on the exiting hordes and hop-scotched down the stairs.

David moved slowly, carefully after him. His mind was occupied with vivid memories of Elizabeth's husband, shriveled and dying, of crippled children, hungry starvelings anxiously depicted on posters appealing for donations. He watched the mothers push the wheelchairs on to the next attraction. Poignant parade of pathos, it hurt him to watch.

"Did you hear what I said?" Rebecca demanded.

"No," he answered, and kept mostly silent for the rest of the day.

They went to the dolphin show, the Dancing Waters, and they took time to visit the open tanks where tourists could pet the whales and porpoises. The creatures felt like cold, slimy rubber—oddly stiff for such supple animals.

Jason claimed his skateboard, and they drove back to the hotel in tired quietude.

Everyone took a nap.

David's sleep was deep and dreamless.

When he awoke, a hushed contentment had come over him, despite its laconic and taciturn beginnings.

He took them to a local haven called the Spice Rack, where tanned and mellow beach children served up summer salads and vegetarian casseroles with the lassitude of lazy, restful vacationers.

It was a pleasant uneventful dinner. The heat of the day had lulled them all into a neutral mood—not completely insipid, but lackluster and opaque. He paid the waitress with a credit card and spent several minutes in the haggle of proper identification. It seemed to take her an interminable amount of time to take the card and run it through the machine. He suggested reading the numbers to her, but she told him that her boss didn't think that was cool.

He was tempted to interrogate her about what possible relation his legal documents could have to the vocabulary of temperature, but he resisted the urge, since his mood basked in a calm that her sluggishness had not disturbed in any significant way.

"What do you say we take a leisurely stroll along the boardwalk of Mission Beach?"

"Cool," Jason perked up.

"Why not?" was Rebecca's contribution.

The cement sidewalk in that part of the city stretches for miles along the length of the peninsula that forms Mission Beach. A sea wall has been constructed to hold back the angry swells during winter storms. The nest of little beach houses that are crowded together like tenements depend on the wall's protection from flooding.

During the temperate months, the sea wall serves as a social club, a welcoming bench where people gather to chat over cans of Coors or carefully rolled joints. The streetlights stay lit all night, providing warmth and illumination for the night owls and insomniacs who hover nearby and greet the sunrise.

Teenagers on roller skates whiz along the sidewalk dodging sailors on leave who walk in unison seeking action. Longhairs and bikers cluster around, checking things out and not saying much. Couples walk arm in arm, and winos pass their bottles around to minors and stoned college kids who regard mingling with this curious underbelly of society as a cultural experience.

Tourists pour in by the hundreds to ogle this community where the cops are known by their first names and the stewardesses who live at the south end have a speaking acquaintance with the barkers from Belmont Park.

Jason took off on his skateboard, tossing a quick "Catch you later, dude" to his father, who walked along unhurriedly drinking in the sights of the street theater.

Rebecca kept pace with her father.

Scores of people passed them going in both directions. Adolescents in bright costumes laughed in careless waves at the comical nature of the pretty people on parade.

Gangs of savory-looking bodies, tan and lithe and beautiful, walked along intoxicated with their carefree, seemingly uncomplicated lives.

The women were blond and luscious, with muscular calves that suggested exercise, voices that sounded like money, and movements that implied they were used to being admired.

Rebecca watched her father contemplate, examine, and scrutinize them for every alluring, pleasing detail.

He found them appealing; she was sure of that.

"I could never be like they are," she confessed unexpectedly.

He turned to the dark child walking at his side.

"And aren't you glad? You're just fine the way you are."

26

The tower of Balboa Park's Museum of Man rises majestically through a clot of elegant eucalyptus trees growing defiantly in the rusty, arid soil.

They had crossed the bridge high atop the freeway below, where streams of weekend-morning traffic zigzagged every which way through the park. David noticed that iron grills had been welded atop the cement walls.

Jason had inquired about them. David said he could only assume they'd been placed there to keep people from jumping. Jason had reflected on that for an instant, then taken off on his skateboard.

"Well so much for the question-and-answer period," Rebecca huffed.

"Not all of us are preoccupied with the sullen and morose."

"Is that supposed to mean I am?"

"Not at all."

"Well, I do think about death. Not all the time, but I've thought about it."

"And what have you concluded?"

"That it's terrible."

He smiled knowingly at her, which she misinterpreted as mockery.

"Well, it is, goddamn it! It's a gyp! You spend all your time trying to accomplish something, except for the imbeciles who don't care about anything, and just when things should be good, you crump. It's disgusting."

"At best, it is violently unfair. All paths of glory lead but to the grave. . . ."

"It makes you wonder why anybody bothers to do anything."

"Most people don't."

"Still, I suppose the ones who do are fighting back, in a way."

"You mean preserving a sense of immortality?"

"Reminding people that they were around, yes."

"I think that's why most people have children."

She didn't press him for further elaboration.

They climbed the stairs to look at the new Old Globe, now risen from the ashes of arson and in the process of being redecorated by eager philanthropists and interested businesses. He brought Rebecca a T-shirt with Shakespeare's picture on the chest.

What had fascinated David most about the arson was the convoluted psyche of the woman who had allegedly struck the match. He read in a newspaper account displayed in an exhibit at the theater that the suspect had worked as a nightwatch. A lonely job, he mused. He had pondered her motivations as a serious, philosophical question. It was the gap in logic that had so intrigued him. Why burn the Old Globe? Why not a library, a house, a boutique that sold imported furniture? He had decided that she had lit the match not to deprive a city of Elizabethan drama but to remind the population that she existed as a force to be reckoned with. Her name had gotten into the newspapers, the court records, the hospital, the jail. She had received hate mail and, he was certain, a few fan letters from other anonymous lonely-hearts. A stir had been created around her, a flutter of activity—most of it hostile, but never mind.

She had made her charred mark.

Fought back, and was mostly forgotten.

He felt that he understood her.

They ate their lunch at the Café del Rey Moro, outside on the tiled patio in the midst of the flora and fauna of a tropical garden. Birds of paradise and elephant ears sprouted and bloomed in the dark soil where Boston ferns thrived despite the heat.

He'd settled three arguments that morning. A grainy fatigue had edged its way behind his eyes. Jason had been upset when David had sided with his sister, then Rebecca pouted when he took Jason's defense in some already forgotten issue.

He mapped out his plan in one solid strategy.

They would eat, go to the zoo, and drive back home.

He watched the people in the café set about their lunches. Romantic couples huddled together at small tables bordering the colorful garden. He speculated that they were swimming in love's beginnings, agog with the promises of oneness, intimacy that belonged to them alone, the private tenderness so unique to the onset of deep feelings. He was sad that they would drown in love's debris, go down in a flood of ugly accusations, hurtful tirades of the other's inadequacies, and be shook by the final, solemn death knell that perhaps it had never been as imagined.

He researched the elderly, their wizened faces chewing in small bites and keeping conversation to a pleasant minimum. He wanted to vault up and ask them if they were happy—did they still wait for the morning, did they regret anything, were they afraid of dying, and would they please tell him, after all those years, what love is?

"This ice cream tastes like Raid!"

"Then don't eat it."

"But that's wasteful."

"So what?"

"I thought waste distressed you."

"Aw, man, just eat it or shut up, will you?"

Rebecca continued to stare at David, waiting for an answer that didn't come.

"Well?" she insisted.

"Well, what?"

"You said that waste distressed you."

"So I did, Rebecca. That was in reference to conspicuous consumption, not one lone bowl of ice cream. I'd like to get moving."

"Are we still going to the zoo?" asked Jason, treading cautiously around his father's foul humor.

"Yes," he uttered without much enthusiasm.

"Good, he can ogle his ancestors," Rebecca chirped.

"They don't have a dog pen for yours, scuz bag."

"What I'm hoping for," said David, addressing them both rather loudly, "is an isolation chamber for weary parents."

His tone put them on alert to cease fire. Rebecca made a point to walk ahead of them just far enough so they couldn't hear her acrimonious mutters in response to her brother's inanity.

She scanned the lovely panorama of the park and thought about her mother. The natural history museum looked like what she imagined a European library to be, with its wide marble steps bookended by two majestic stone lions. The Reuben H. Fleet Space Theater and Science Center stood out in clashing juxtaposition to the architecture of the rest of the building.

She preferred a certain symmetry to things. Even the books in her room were lined up in order—properly, as she liked to think of it.

They rounded the corner past the puppet theater and the Mexican village, a cluster of minuscule art studios. And then they were at the zoo.

David bought the tickets, and the three of them solemnly pushed their way through the turnstile. On either side of the entryway stood two busts of ferocious gorillas carved in black iron and scowling a fierce welcome.

He did not ask but announced to his charges how the day would go.

"First we are going to take the bus tour for an overall picture, then we can revisit areas of interest, after which we will go to the children's zoo, pet the bloody animals, and get the hell out of here. Am I being clear enough?"

"Right on, dude," Jason saluted him. Rebecca nodded sullenly.

They waddled over to the flamingo pond and boarded the next bus that came along.

A chipper fellow in a khaki uniform sat in the driver's seat with a microphone attached to his lapel and a stack of Wonder Bread neatly piled on the dashboard.

"Good afternoon, ladies and gentlemen," he intoned, his nasal twang singing into the mike as he accelerated the open-air trolley down the road to rare birds in tightly constructed cages. He gave short, informative orations, precision timed with jokes carefully constructed to embrace all ages.

They swung down to the hippos and the lions, the bears and the sea otters. He drove them past giraffes, mountain goats, penguins in icy cages, koalas in leafy trees, and camels slinking over arid terrain.

On the whole, it was pretty impressive. Jason hung out the side of the bus and whistled to the animals he found fascinating.

Rebecca sat quietly in her seat, blatantly ignoring everyone, but he could tell she was listening to the guide. She double-checked his information on the well-indicated signs posted by each cage. He caught her laughing at a lazy polar bear, too phlegmatic to get up and chase the bread thrown to him.

Instead, this ursine monster rolled onto his massive back and fanned out his paws as if lying spread-eagled on a beach in Mazatlán.

He bought them all snow cones and opened it up to a vote.

"Let's go cruise the snakes!"

"You cruise the snakes. Those slithery mothers make me sick."

"Well, what do you want to see, Rebecca?"

"The monkeys."

"Figures," Jason sneered. She did not give him the benefit of a response.

"Fair is fair. Jason, you go to the herpetology section. Rebecca, you hit the primates. We will meet back here in *exactly* twenty minutes. Any questions?"

"What's herpatchoulli?"

"Snakes, stupid."

"Go," David commanded them abruptly.

Jason jogged off toward the glass enclosure that housed vipers and pythons, killers, and household pets.

Rebecca walked slowly past the gigantic cages wired tightly together for the monkeys. He followed her for no specific reason.

She paused in front of a cage where several frisky spider monkeys chased each other around in a riot of passion, up and down the walls, over to the trapeze and into the water bin. One playful fellow picked up a dried apple and pitched it at the onlookers on the other side of the cage.

He could see her lips curl in amusement at his audacity.

She saw him, but said nothing.

In the corner of the cafe a mother monkey nursed a tiny one, her arms wrapped tightly around its diminutive body as she held it close. In the plaintive look on her face glared a tender determination. At her side stood the father monkey, poised and tense, watchful for any trouble. One of his paws rested gently on the mother's back.

He did not know why, but he did recall most clearly the monkey's stare as Rebecca turned to him suddenly, her eyes brimming with unexpected tears. A wail not unlike a coyote's shrieked up from her throat.

"Why ever did you leave us like that?"

And as gently and concisely as he could manage, he told her, as best he knew how.

"When you and Jason were born, I was so scared."

"Of what?"

"Of your mother not loving me."

"You thought she wouldn't love you because of us?"

"Yes. I didn't know how to share."

"Did you try?"

"I really wanted to try, but I was too selfish to love you, and I left," he confessed nervously.

She pondered that for a moment.

"I came back to see if I could learn to love. I'm not terribly good at it."

A tense silence filled the space between them as Rebecca studied his face for smirks or lies.

"Are you going to leave me again?"

"I have to go back to Boston, if that's what you're asking."

"What happens now?"

"I don't know, Rebecca."

He would have liked to come up with a better answer, solid proof, hard evidence where no room for doubt was allowed.

But he didn't have one to give her.

"We'll just all have to see, Rebecca."

27

They had spread the entire Sunday edition of the *Los Angeles Times* over the living room floor, eaten bagels and cream cheese, drunk coffee from Bay Cities, and gone back to bed.

She had even joined him for a jog on the beach, after which they had gone for a swim.

It had been a pleasant weekend, nervous at first, but bit by bit they had eased back into the cozy familiarity of reading each other's moods out of habit and responding with the comfort that comes from years spent coping together.

They talked of vacation plans. He told her about a new client in the works.

She detailed the plans for *Iceman*'s set.

Both of them rather missed the presence of the children, though they did not mention it.

Sam would drift over to the window just to peek and see if the rented car was on its way up the hill.

From time to time Roger descended into the garage, looking down the road before grabbing a tool or putting something in the car.

Roland called.

The mirrors for Harry Hope's bar had arrived cracked. The flats for the Raines-Law section of the hotel were done and looked pretty good.

"Just flecked enough to be violently depressing, dearie."

Someone was working on the food, which would be made of plaster of paris or Play-Doh.

"We have to make it look mummified ham-and-cheese, dumplin'. For that we could order out to about a dozen restaurants I could name."

Part of the set called for a tattered ebony curtain to serve as a room divider. He had agreed to take care of it.

"I'm telling you, Sam, you don't have to look very far for filthy linen. About half of this building's laundry would qualify for props in a slum dwelling. I'm serious, pet; you could die from the pigs around here."

"Did you get it?" Sam yawned into the phone. She had no reason to be tired, yet her body felt heavy with languor of Sunday sluggishness.

"Carl dyed a flat sheet in the washer. Turned out okay, but we'll have to dirty it up a little."

"Sounds good."

"What, the dirtying up?"

"Roland?"

"Oui, cupcake?"

"Bye."

"Tell me, precious, did that cur bring back the beasties yet?"

"No, not yet."

"Consider yourself blessed, then. Perhaps he'll try and whisk them away to Boston. Lucky you."

"I doubt it."

"Me too, angel. He's nobody's fool."

"Roland, you give me a headache."

"The truth shall set your free! Isn't that the most *loathsome* lie? I want deception, illusion, and dreams, thank you very much."

"Right."

"I never lied in my heart—au contraire, I *always* lie in my heart. What better place for falsehood, I ask you?"

"Bye, Roland."

"Ta-ta, tulip."

He's a decent enough person, she thought to herself. Hysterical, efficient, a dreadfully dramatic guy, but a good one. He'd hired her when she was desperate and depressed, convinced her to keep pushing despite insufferable odds, including two children he could scarcely tolerate.

Her gratitude had gradually evolved into a friendship that thrived on crisis alternating with interludes of tranquil uneventfulness.

"Who was that?" Roger asked, looking up from a pile of forms he'd been wading through.

"That was the Song of Roland," she said, and added, "he sends his love."

"Terrific," he replied, raising his eyebrows ever so slightly.

He liked Roland well enough. He had been Roger's first exposure to a homosexual outside of cheap jokes and random accusations.

At first he'd been slightly ill at ease—fearful actually; he didn't know what to expect. In his ignorance he'd imagined that Roland felt bad that he looked married and normal.

That got settled early.

They had been invited out to dinner to celebrate Roland's anniversary. Roger had simply assumed that the festivities centered around his successful years in the theater.

But he had been mistaken.

Their convivial repast at Ma Maison had been to rejoice at his nine-year union with Carl.

It had been quite an occasion. Everyone drank too much and talked guardedly and awkwardly until Roger had raised his glass for a toast and stammered, "I don't know what to say."

Roland had picked up his long-stemmed crystal goblet and suggested, "Why don't you just say, 'Much happiness to a couple a' winsome faggots?' "

And they had laughed at the absurdity of their nervousness, and that was the end of that.

David glided the car carefully through the congested lanes of traffic heading toward Los Angeles.

"Where have all these people been?" he inquired of anyone who would answer.

"Baja," Jason offered.

"What do they do down there?"

"They cruise it on the dunes."

He turned to Rebecca, who sat huddled against the door staring off at the vast terrain of Camp Pendleton.

"Translation?"

"They go down to Mexico with these dune buggies, tear up the land, swill down cases of beer, and act just as stupid as they do at home, except they wear shorts."

"Aw, man, you rip everything! Lance's dad has a hot dune buggy. They go down there almost every weekend."

"Lance's father is an android."

"He is not!"

"Okay, then, he's only a troglodyte."

"You make me sick."

"Whatever," she sighed, and turned to gaze at San Clemente.

He was bone weary by now; there was not enough force in him to settle disputes, break up brawls, or even lecture on the benefits of peaceful coexistence.

All the way to Santa Monica he thought about Boston, pausing only to answer Jason's questions.

Rebecca had turned silent, her eyes glued on the stretch of freeway before them.

He didn't attempt to draw her out.

It was dusk by the time they got home. The sun was setting over the calm of the Pacific, a flaming red ball sinking into the flat, azure horizon. The air was pungent with odors of seaweed and brine.

"They're home!" Samantha jumped out and raced to open the front door. A beacon of light shone down the steps.

"Hi, Mom, Dad!" Jason shrieked.

"Hi, sweetie. Did you have a good time?"

"Killer," he yelled, and vaulted the stairs two at a time. He left all of his luggage in the car. Rebecca took hers, refusing assistance from anyone.

"Well, we're home," was her greeting and salutation.

Roger joined Sam at the door as David struggled up the stairs with Jason's things. He hoped the son of a bitch had spent a miserable weekend. He studied his face for signs of fatigue. Thank God he was going back to Boston. Roger hated the entire East Coast, a dirty, polluted cement jungle full of dog shit and pretensions. A perfect place for this guy to live, he concluded.

"Come on in, David," he said casually.

"Well, how'd it go?" Sam asked with interest.

"All in all, we managed fairly well."

He set down the suitcases and felt the whoosh of wind on his back as Roger closed the front door.

"Drink? You look like you could use one."

David sighed heavily and observed all of them standing there together.

"Actually, I think I'll be shoving off, but thanks just the same, for everything."

The moment ached with stiffness.

"Look, I'm not much good at long good-byes, so I think I'll just say it and take off."

Roger moved toward him and extended his hand.

"Good-bye, David."

Next, David looked to Sam, who eyed him with a wizened tenderness and hugged him close to her for an instant.

"Please keep in touch, David."

"I intend to," was his whispered response. She smiled at him sadly and moved back next to Roger, who put his arm around her shoulder.

Jason flew into his arms and gave him a strong hug and a wet kiss.

"Hey, dude, it's been a blast. Will you come back?"

"Perhaps."

"Well," and he let his thumb and his pinky extend themselves fully and twisted his wrist back and forth.

"Shaka brah, dude." He grinned from ear to ear and gave his own definition. "That's Hawaiian for good-bye. Teach it to the snowballs in your class."

"I'll do that."

Rebecca stood still and sullen near the door. Her eyes scanned the tile of the entryway as if she were searching for some minute lost object.

"Rebecca." She looked up and stared at him coldly.

He moved toward her, his arms open and ready for a hug. Instead she extended her hand and allowed him to shake it.

"I may or may not write to you," she announced to him matter-of-factly. "It's a decision I intend to make at a later date."

"Good-bye, Rebecca."

She nodded that she had heard him.

He did not look back as he went down the stairs to his car.

He sat in the driveway for a while, thinking that perhaps Rebecca would come to him but she didn't. The light on the stairs went out, and sadly he turned on the ignition.

28

The congestion at the air-
port had surprised him.
He double-checked to verify that he was in the right
terminal.

Someone kicked his baggage accidentally as he consulted his tickets, and the clasp gave way. Bales of dirty
laundry rolled onto the floor as more passengers traipsed
through, oblivious to the scattered garments.

"Son of a bitch," he mumbled through the tickets in
his teeth, as he amassed his soiled belongings as best he
could.

"The sooner I get out of this place the better," he
muttered to the strangers milling around him.

"Miss?" he asked a Hertz lady, thinking her to work
for the airlines. "Where's American's flight 2?"

"How am I supposed to know?" she answered
bluntly.

A man carrying double briefcases stopped to help him.

"Flight 2 to Boston? Over here."

David followed him through the crowded terminal, where he spotted the check-in counter with the comfortingly familiar logo.

He checked his luggage and asked for a seat in the smoking section.

"Have a nice flight," the woman wished him.

"Don't worry," he said, but he didn't push it.

He made his way to gate 7, stopping off at the gift shop to buy a *New York Times,* a real newspaper at last.

Passengers for Boston were scattered about the black vinyl chairs, waiting to board. A quick inventory revealed no babies or small children who might be on his flight. He relaxed a little. Snatches of conversation assailed his ears as he looked for a seat.

The refreshing rudeness of New Yorkers' terse, clipped diction delighted him. He could overhear the cadence of a money deal being rehashed in detail in the long and whiny vowels of Brooklyn. Transplanted New Yorkers added to the appeal of Boston. He saw them as the levelers of blue-blood pretension, and he loved them for it.

The flight crew was preparing to board, attractive men and women dragging metal trolleys with matching luggage. He guessed them all to be in their early thirties, so different from the youngsters who used to fly for the glamour of it.

The women were better-looking than the men, he judged after careful consideration.

He spotted one he wouldn't mind knowing.

He made a mental note to introduce himself to the willowy blonde.

He had made himself a promise. He would think of nothing serious until the plane was safely in the air and he had consumed at least two very strong scotch and waters.

Then and only then would he review the events of the past month.

He'd given himself permission to become sentimental, if only for a little while, but it was not yet time for that.

The passengers were called to board. He took one last look around, decided that the carpet needed cleaning, and entered the plane.

"Hi," he said to the blond beauty who tore his ticket and showed him his seat. Her regard was one of interest, he was quick to remark.

He stored his hand luggage and buckled himself into the seat.

She cruised the aisles with graceful ease, making sure each seat belt was fastened and each chair was upright.

David kept his eyes on what he judged to be exceptionally beautiful legs as the comely blonde moved closer to his seat.

"Are you David Bartholomew?"

"In the flesh," he replied seductively.

"I have something for you."

"I was rather hoping you'd say that."

She reached inside her jacket pocket and handed him an envelope—containing, he was certain, her address and phone number. He smiled coyly, thinking how much the role of women had changed, from waiting passively to offering aggressively.

"This is from a girl in a Shakespeare T-shirt who seemed most anxious that you receive it."

She had moved on to the rear of the cabin before he

could comment. The roar of the engines accelerated into the dull whine of propulsion as the loudspeaker instructed the crew to prepare for takeoff.

He looked at the envelope with no stamp, no address, just his name in bold, courageous print. He ripped it open, glancing briefly at the salutation to make sure there was no mistake. He could feel the agitation swell in him as he studied the page and took in its contents.

He swallowed and blinked back tears of confusion. He knew all about the complexities of moral choices; after all, he was a scholar who had dissected the great ones and all their ramifications. It annoyed him to think that everyday life could impose such mundane and facile decisions with such urgency, and in the absence of the right circumstances for careful consideration. The irritating beat of his heart quickened and pounded. What he needed was to refind a tranquil peace within himself in order to think things through prudently.

But the airplane was beginning its gentle roll away from the terminal. David glanced from side to side in a maelstrom of anxiety, as if searching for the calming advice of a fellow passenger.

The crew was demonstrating the lifesaving equipment. Soon the Muzak would resume its indifferent melody.

He scanned the bevy of vacant faces and drew one quick breath lest he change his mind. Then he unhitched his safety belt and rose cautiously to his feet.

"Sit down, sir," the flight attendant sporting a Mae West shouted sharply.

"I can't," David said anxiously, allowing himself no time for reflection. He charged toward the exit door, which had already been firmly closed.

"Take your seat, sir!" insisted the head flight attendant, poised by the phone connected to the cockpit.

"Open the door," he demanded coldly.

"We're moving."

"I said open the fucking door!" he shrieked in a voice that alarmed the passengers, who no doubt feared the metal detector had somehow failed to alert officials that a dreaded hijacker was aboard.

"Open it now!" he shouted to the staff and silent attendant, who was phoning the pilot.

Ominous clangs and screeches followed, like lug nuts loose on a wheel.

The aircraft reversed its direction and inched its way back toward the terminal.

He could scarcely contain himself as the harried attendant released the pressure wheel and pushed the door aside on its sloping diagonal.

Officials were standing there, but he pushed past them and jogged through the portable tunnel, which shook under his feet as he fled toward the waiting area.

He scanned the crowded terminal with its hordes of anxious faces waiting for their cues from hidden loudspeakers.

He could not see her anywhere.

He crashed around corners, knocking over aluminum ashtrays and bumping into vinyl chairs lined up in symmetrical rows.

His eyes darted in all directions, searching for a T-shirt, a scowl, a clue.

He spotted her in the distance leaning against a pillar, her arms crossed in hostile anticipation, waiting for him to let her down once again.

He moved toward her slowly, desperately seeking the

right words, the critical phrase that would turn this important moment into one of righteous clarity.

Her face came into focus, and her eyes transformed from angry slits to saucers of disbelief that melted into tears.

He opened his mouth, but before he could utter a sound she had vaulted into his outstretched arms, her ear firmly crushed against his chest, where his heart pulsated in involuntary spasms that sounded something like the beginning of a prayer.